"He's not here."

Roxanne studied each customer in turn. Though the bar boasted several dark-haired men in conservative suits, none of them was Gage. None had his stark masculinity, his sexy— *Whoa. What's this?* She focused on two men at one end of the bar.

"He's there," Roxanne whispered. Her body grew numb and her heart sank as her gaze locked on the familiar sculpted cheekbones and jaw.

Her friend Toni followed her gaze. "I was kind of expecting him to be with a svelte blond lover. Wait, he's got a ponytail! And he's *smoking!*"

Roxanne had noticed that, too. The sophisticated surface she saw every day had been wiped away, as if the charming man she lived with was an act and a dangerous stranger had taken his place.

He'd lied to her. What the hell was going on? In that moment of watching her fiancé acting like someone else…something inside her shifted.

Snapped.

Gage may think he's got me fooled, she thought furiously as she rose from her chair, *but this is where it ends….*

Dear Reader,

Ah, bad boys. Aren't they just sigh-inducingly wonderful?

Though this story opens with Roxanne, to me it will always be Gage's book. This is why the book begins where it does—not with him meeting the woman of his dreams and falling in love, but after he's already popped the question.

"This *is* a romance, right?" you ask.

You betcha. Just an unconventional one. Because things are not what they seem with Gage. He's got secrets. (*Psst*...one really big one.)

I hope you enjoy reading about Gage and his past, his motivations and dreams. And I think you'll find Roxanne grows into his perfect match. But in the meantime he's got a whole lot of explaining to do....

I'd love to hear from you via my Web site: www.wendyetherington.com. Or my mailing address: P.O. Box 3016, Irmo, SC 29063.

Hope much love and laughter comes your way,

Wendy Etherington

PRIVATE LIES
Wendy Etherington

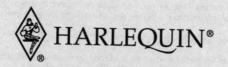

HARLEQUIN®

TORONTO • NEW YORK • LONDON
AMSTERDAM • PARIS • SYDNEY • HAMBURG
STOCKHOLM • ATHENS • TOKYO • MILAN • MADRID
PRAGUE • WARSAW • BUDAPEST • AUCKLAND

To my sisters, Catherine Word and Laura Gurner, for their constant love and support.

ISBN 0-373-69144-0

PRIVATE LIES

Copyright © 2003 by Wendy Etherington.

All rights reserved. Except for use in any review, the reproduction or utilization of this work in whole or in part in any form by any electronic, mechanical or other means, now known or hereafter invented, including xerography, photocopying and recording, or in any information storage or retrieval system, is forbidden without the written permission of the publisher, Harlequin Enterprises Limited, 225 Duncan Mill Road, Don Mills, Ontario, Canada M3B 3K9.

All characters in this book have no existence outside the imagination of the author and have no relation whatsoever to anyone bearing the same name or names. They are not even distantly inspired by any individual known or unknown to the author, and all incidents are pure invention.

This edition published by arrangement with Harlequin Books S.A.

® and TM are trademarks of the publisher. Trademarks indicated with ® are registered in the United States Patent and Trademark Office, the Canadian Trade Marks Office and in other countries.

Visit us at www.eHarlequin.com

Printed in U.S.A.

1

Roxanne Lewis's heart lurched. "It can't be."

Antoinette St. Clair—Toni to all who intended to stay on her good side—lifted her gaze from her plate of salmon. Her eyes filled with regret. "I'm sorry, Rox, but Gage *was* in the Quarter last night."

"He's supposed to be in Chicago."

"He's not."

Tucked in the corner booth of her favorite French Quarter restaurant, away from the curious eyes of the other diners, Roxanne pushed away her nearly untouched crab Louis salad. No one ever accused Toni of being flighty—without acquiring bruises anyway. If she said she saw Gage in New Orleans, she did.

Roxanne fought against the panic fluttering in her stomach, recalling last Saturday night, when she and Gage had eaten a late dinner, when he'd slid his hand along her thigh during dessert...

"Doing what?" she asked quickly, banishing the erotic thoughts.

"Leaning against the wall outside a bar."

Maybe he'd just come back a day early. Maybe he'd had a late business meeting. He'd had a lot of those lately. "Was he with anyone?"

"No, but he studied the crowd a lot and kept glancing at his watch." Toni gestured with her fork. "Like he was waiting for someone."

Someone. Not her. How many times had she wondered what he saw in her? He'd chosen *her*. He'd proposed to *her*. And, yet, insecurity lingered. There were parts of Gage he didn't share with her. She'd tried to tell herself it didn't matter. He showered her with affection, devotion...loyalty. Just because he was sexy as hell, smart and rich didn't mean *every* woman in New Orleans was chasing him.

Only the ones between twenty and sixty.

Roxanne sipped her water and tried to pretend a lump wasn't blocking her throat. "Do you think he could have been meeting a woman?"

"Maybe. God knows I've been tempted."

Roxanne's gaze jumped to Toni's. "To cheat?"

Her friend grinned. "No, to jump Gage Dabon's bones."

"Be serious."

The smile wiped from her face, Toni angled her head. "I am. I'm seriously pissed. Why aren't you?"

"I am." *No, you're not, Roxanne. You're scared. Bone-deep scared. You knew you'd never hold him.*

"Stop." Toni tugged a strand of Roxanne's long, corkscrew-curly red hair. "You're quite a catch yourself, Foxy Roxy."

Roxanne didn't bother to deny Toni had guessed the direction of her thoughts. They'd been friends too long. "He'd be better off with someone like you," Roxanne said. "Someone more outgoing."

"Hell, Rox, we haven't had *near* enough wine for a pity party." She frowned at her water glass. "We haven't had *any* wine." Shrugging, Toni polished off the last bite of her salmon, then handed her plate to a passing waiter. "And, no offense, but Gage's too tame for me. Hunky, yes. But banks, blue suits and dark ties? No, thanks."

You haven't seen that body without the suits. Then the implication of Toni's words sunk in. "I like tame. There's nothing wrong with tame."

"That's because you grew up with excitement, not Miss Manners lessons twenty-four hours a day."

Roxanne didn't want to go anywhere near the subject of Toni's intimidating, uptight mother. Talk about scary.

Thankfully, Toni tucked a strand of her shaggy blond hair behind her ear and rolled on. "And, speaking of annoying relatives, you have to remember the way Gage stood up under your family's scrutiny. Any man who'd do that has to want you pretty badly."

"True." Roxanne's father, brother and sister were all cops. Nobel, brave and strong. They stood for the weak and defenseless; they worked tirelessly so other families could be spared the kind of tragedy that Roxanne's had suffered—her mother dying at the hands of a paroled murderer, who'd sought to punish Roxanne's father for sending him to prison.

Roxanne had felt abandoned without her mother and had no desire to run into the kind of people who had killed her. Accounting, not law enforcement was her calling. Numbers didn't lie, numbers made sense...numbers didn't die.

Wimpy, her sister had once accused. Practical, Roxanne had argued back. Of course, practicality was obviously missing from every Lewis's genetic makeup except hers.

"So, what's the plan?" Toni asked, leaning forward, her blue eyes twinkling with anticipation.

"What plan? I'll ask him what he was doing in the Quarter last night and why he didn't bother to call me. Or come home."

Toni tapped her long, acrylic nails—currently painted hot pink with green palm trees and bright yellow suns on each one in anticipation of the busy summer-tourist season—against the table. "Uh-huh. You? Miss Nonconfrontation. *You're* going to ask Gage why he lied, who he was meeting."

"Yes." She banged her fist against the table, knowing she needed this pep talk to urge her on. "Do you think I should act angry and demand an answer, or be sly and attempt to catch him lying?"

"You've already caught him in a lie, and I think you should *be* angry."

"I am."

"Then why are your hands shaking?"

Sighing, Roxanne immediately linked her fingers. "I can't help it. I won't know what to say."

"Where the hell were you last night, you lying bastard? works for me."

"Be reasonable, Toni."

"Why?"

Roxanne rubbed her temples, unable to come up with a reasonable argument at the moment. She'd no doubt think of something hours from now, but the impact would be lost. How did people train themselves to think on their feet? After a lifetime of friendship with Toni, shouldn't some of her sass have rubbed off?

"Since you don't have a plan, mine is perfect."

Roxanne instinctively shook her head. Oh, no. Toni's past plans had included everything from giving the dog the keys to her mother's brand-new Mercedes—which he'd promptly buried in the back-yard—to sawing off the legs of Sister Margaretta's desk in the seventh grade, to disguising the two of them in black wigs and red lipstick to sneak into fraternity parties at Tulane.

As usual, Toni ignored Roxanne's protest. "I think we should follow him."

"No." If Toni was surprised by her direct, one-word refusal, she didn't show it. And, dang it, she'd been practicing.

"You have a right to know what's going on," Toni continued.

"I will. I'll ask."

"And if he denies it?"

"I'll—" She stopped, breaking her friend's direct glare. Gage was smooth, sometimes almost too smooth. Roxanne had no doubt the man could say he'd been called into New Orleans for an hour, then directed back to Mars, and somehow effectively convince her that was the absolute and complete truth.

"Come on, Rox. We'll disguise ourselves. It'll be just like college. I've got the perfect disguise picked out at the shop already."

The shop—aka the Tacky Diva. When she'd attended the splashy opening of Toni's store, Roxanne was sure Toni had used her trust fund to open the lingerie, costume and party-clothes store just to piss off her conservative family. But her friend's shop had survived for nearly ten years and was now courted by the trust-fund babies for ammunition in catching the perfect husband, then those same women shopped for their wedding trousseaux.

Roxanne often wondered how many seasoned

trust-fund lawyers blanched at the Visa charges from the Tacky Diva, instead of Saks.

"No disguises," she said firmly—she'd been practicing that tone. "No following. No videotaping. No tracking devices. No bugs."

"Why the hell not? You have a right to the truth."

"A sentiment undoubtedly not shared by Sister Katherine after you bugged her office phone, then told our tenth-grade English class she'd been dialing 1–900–HUNKMAN in her spare time."

"I can get a bug so small it'll slide alongside the battery of his cell phone."

Roxanne's stomach rolled. This morning she'd been blissfully happy, planning her wedding, and now she was contemplating bugging her fiancé's cell phone? "No. And isn't bugging someone's property without their knowledge, or a court order, illegal?"

"Why in the world would you bug someone *with* their knowledge?"

"I—" That girl was nearly as slick as Gage. Roxanne fought hard against the urge to run back to her office and hide under the desk until this whole storm passed. She didn't want to spy on her lover. She didn't want to confront him. She wanted...

To be a fool.

"Just think about my idea," Toni said, her usually animated face dead serious. "Remember, with my plan you can avoid confronting him for the moment. You can find out the truth." She squeezed Roxanne's hand in a gesture of complete fidelity and understanding. "You *deserve* the truth."

"I know, but—"

"Speak of the devil." Toni leaned back against the

red, leather-covered booth. Her face relaxed, but her eyes narrowed at a spot over Roxanne's shoulder.

Roxanne didn't have to glance back to know who'd entered the restaurant, but she did anyway, unable to resist the temptation of simply watching Gage Dabon move.

She turned in time to see the maître d' pointing out her table. Gage's broad shoulders and trim physique were encased in an expensive-looking dark blue suit. His gorgeous, sculpted face and his confident, almost arrogant manner—no doubt delivered to him via his Creole ancestors—caused more than a few heads to turn. His thick, slightly wavy hair gleamed blue-black under the crystal chandeliers, as if an enhancing spotlight followed every step he took, every muscle he flexed. He moved with purpose, with an almost predatory gait. Nothing would sway him from his path. Deny him what he sought.

What the hell was he doing with *her?* she wondered, and not for the first time.

"Oh, God," she said in a low tone to Toni. "I'm not ready to face him."

"Be strong. I'm here. Ask him where he went to dinner last night."

"Afternoon, babe."

Roxanne reached deep for some Lewis nerves and lifted her face for Gage's light kiss. His lips lingered just a bit on hers, longer than was really appropriate for lunchtime affection. But then they hadn't seen each other in four days, and their reunions weren't usually so public.

She craved him with a hunger that had everything

to do with sexual need, and yet she knew there was so much more.

"I missed you," he said against her lips.

As always, the wonder of his touch and his voice exploded in her stomach, rolled through her blood, making her glad she was sitting, as her knees would never hold her weight. He stroked her jaw with his thumb, his silvery gaze meeting hers. "You look tired. Not sleeping well without me?"

Lack of sleep was the least of her troubles. Her stomach clenched. "I'm fine."

He continued to stare at her for the space of two heartbeats, as if deciding whether or not to accept her answer, but obviously choosing not to push. He glanced across the table. "Hello, Toni. I'm pleased to see someone can convince her to take time for lunch."

He's so cool, Roxanne thought, watching him unbutton his suit coat and slide into the booth next to her. Was he cool enough to lie to her? And why? Would he really betray her with another woman?

Her heart raced. Nervous, she fiddled with a napkin rolled up in a place setting, finally pushing it and her plate in front of Gage. "Have you eaten?"

He regarded the plate, then her. "No, and you haven't either."

"You have it."

"Fine. We'll share." He dropped the napkin on his lap then forked up a bite of crab, holding it in front of her lips.

Knowing it never did any good to argue with Gage, Roxanne took the bite. His thigh brushed hers, and their intimate position reminded her of other nudges and sighs, erotic moments, familiar touches. She swallowed crab she didn't taste, forcing it down with the tears clogging her chest.

"How's business, Toni?"

"Busy. Everybody's gearing up for summer."

"I see more withdrawals than deposits. Not you, though?"

Toni fiddled with the stem of her water glass. "Clients are in the buying mood. In fact, I met with one last night." She paused, her blue eyes cold. "In the Quarter."

Roxanne could have sworn Gage flinched.

Then, a second later, slick as spit, he casually held another bite of salad against her lips. Her heart hammering, her mind buzzing with the answer he might give, she shook her head and leaned back.

One dark eyebrow quirked at the distance she formed between them, and she held her breath for his answer.

His gaze flicked to Toni. "I'll bet things are wild down there."

Roxanne gripped the table in an effort to interrupt, to accuse him of knowing exactly how the Quarter was last night. But she held her tongue.

Maybe because Toni had stamped on her foot.

"I keep my distance at night usually. Though Rox and I like that new restaurant on St. Ann. Maybe we'll go next week." His gaze, full of sincere invitation, locked with hers. "Want to, Rox?"

Roxanne's body ceased beating, moving, or thumping. *He'd lied.* He'd just lied to her face.

A hollow sense of betrayal invaded her.

The waiter set café au lait in front of them, and Roxanne sipped, though she tasted nothing.

Under the table, Toni kicked her. Her friend had, no doubt, sensed the way of the wind. "How was Chicago?" she forced herself to ask.

Gage smiled, his even white teeth flashing beneath the antique lamplights in the restaurant. "Cold as hell. Guess they don't realize it's May up there."

"But no delays," Toni asked, her smile tight as Roxanne's heart restarted and threatened to jump from her chest. "You were able to take off this morning?"

"Smooth takeoff, for which I was glad. I was anxious to get back to Roxanne."

Roxanne noticed he didn't deny taking off this morning. Nor did he exactly confirm. The vagueness bothered her, and she fought to remember other trips and itineraries he might have vaguely mentioned. He'd gone to New York a couple of weeks ago, said he'd be there for two days and wound up staying for four. Had there been other trips she'd blown off as insignificant business meetings and delays? How deep did this go? *How long has the lying been going on?*

Nauseous, she realized Toni had been right. She deserved the truth. She *had* to find out what was happening.

Gage angled his body toward her. "Unfortunately, we're going to have to change our plans for tonight. An unexpected meeting has come up."

Another lie? What is he really doing? And with whom?

"Really?" she asked, working for curious innocence—her usual mentality, so surely she'd pulled it off. "You just got back. I really wanted to share this new restaurant with you. It's a client of mine's first leap into the business. He needs the support."

"I know it was important." His voice deepened

with concern, and he moved closer, angling his body toward hers, effectively boxing her between the wall and his broad chest. His spicy scent invaded her. She fought the urge to touch him. He had a great body. A responsive body.

"I'll make it up to you next week, I promise," he said. "This meeting couldn't be avoided. I'll be in town, but I have to stay over at the hotel."

"Mmm." She glanced at Toni, who sipped her coffee as if she didn't have every molecule directed at their conversation. "Which hotel?"

"The Sheraton."

"Good choice. They have a view of the river, you know. It's—"

"Are you planning to surprise me and show up in my room—" he paused, his grin blooming with devilish enthusiasm, his voice lowering "—naked, perhaps?"

Startled, she raised her head.

He leaned forward, pressing a light kiss on her jaw, sending heat soaring through her veins. "As much as I would enjoy it, you would, no doubt, shock the accounts manager I'm rooming with right out of his Jockey shorts."

She fought desperately against his allure—the spicy, male smell of him, his warm breath against her skin—reminding herself he'd never roomed with anyone before. A very smooth and flattering response to keep her from showing up unexpectedly at his hotel? She never would have considered interrupting his business meetings before today. Before he'd lied.

Her head ached from the unanswered questions, but she swallowed her fear and anger for the moment.

She needed time to figure out what to do, how to confront him.

"I promise not to stay more than two nights," he continued, "and I'll have my cell phone if you need me." His hand slid up her leg, encountering bare flesh at the edge of her thigh-high hose. "God, do you know how sexy these things are?" He whispered. "How am I going to concentrate on stock portfolios now?"

With his clever fingers dancing their way to her crotch, Roxanne drew a deep breath. Damp heat flooded her panties. The tip of his finger brushed the satin, and she squirmed on the seat, wondering how she could discreetly press his hand harder against her. Four nights without him, and she was panting. It was crazy. It was exhilarating.

The pleasure he always brought her was so intense, so powerful, she couldn't doubt his feelings for her, his love for her. Though he rarely said the words out loud. And the concentration and attention he lavished on her had led to security, to trust. Until now. Until doubt and fear and suspicion had reared their ugly heads.

"This is a great chance for a girls' night out. Right, Rox?"

Toni's cheerful but tight voice broke through Roxanne's sexual fantasy. Caught somewhere between wanting, fulfillment, and disappointment at her own needs, she yanked her navy jacket straight and prayed Gage would find that coolness of his, so as not to betray what was actually going on beneath the linen tablecloth.

She need not have worried.

Gage glided his hand from between her thighs to

the small of her back. "I'm glad you'll have Toni to distract you."

"Oh, yeah. We can always troll the bars in the Quarter," Toni said sharply.

Gage's silver eyes flashed with humor. He grinned as his gaze slid from Toni to Roxanne. "Just remember who you belong to, babe," he said lightly.

I remember. Do you? She searched his face for signs of insincerity, for slyness or an outright lie. She saw nothing but warmth and hunger. Directed at her. Gage had that power. He made her feel as if no other woman existed. No man had ever given her that, even her father. Maybe she was addicted to that feeling. Maybe that feeling had led her to believe she was in love. But how could she love a man she didn't really know?

She forced a smile to her lips. "You, of course."

"I need to get going." Gage slid one hand around Roxanne's neck and drew her close. "Think of me."

He pressed his lips briefly to hers, glided out of the booth, then left.

Roxanne sank her teeth into her bottom lip. She wanted him to wrap her in his strong arms almost as much as she wanted to strangle the man.

"So," Toni began, peeking slyly over her coffee cup. "You want to meet me at the shop at three?"

"Definitely."

GAGE DABON STRODE into the Bayou Palace's lobby bar. Checking his Rolex, he sat on a stool and ordered Jack Daniel's—Black Label. He retrieved a sterling-silver case from inside his jacket pocket and, lighting a cigarette, settled back with his drink to wait.

Image was everything in his business, as he'd learned a thousand times over. Image and guts. They kept the deal together. They kept you alive.

As he discreetly scanned the lobby for his quarry, he tried to force his thoughts away from Roxanne. But regret fought its way in.

He hated lying to her, hated it more every day, and the deception made him all the more conscious of how long he'd been at the game and how easy leaving would be. But he couldn't let her discover the truth yet—for her own safety and his. He didn't think she would appreciate the irony of her being engaged to the one kind of man she always said she could never live with—a cop.

Not just any beat cop, either. A Secret Service undercover agent for the United States Treasury Department.

He smiled grimly. No, he'd lose her. And that was unacceptable.

It had begun with an addiction to their favorite restaurant, and now, was he addicted to her as well? Her smile, her touch?

The fact that he'd actually proposed should tell him he'd lost his mind as well as his edge. A wife and a family made you vulnerable, prevented your heart from turning to steel, forced you think about going too far. But he desperately wanted that life with Roxanne.

Her sweetness and purity were like a balm to a man who'd lived among, then tracked and captured, the worst of society for nearly ten years. She made him feel clean when he was so damn tired of being dirty.

Every day he thought more about retiring. Every

time he had to leave her. Every time he had to lie. If he could get through this case...

He shook aside the thought and swallowed another sip of liquor, the drink burning down his throat. He frankly hated the stuff, but the image required it. He had to focus on now. Today. This moment. For now, their engagement bound her to him. He'd find a way to explain things to her soon.

Finally, he spotted his target. And the ridiculous idiocy of criminals struck him anew. The kid—turning twenty-two next month—was a brilliant computer engineer. MIT graduate. Affluent upbringing. All-American good looks—though he really should get to know Calvin Klein and ditch the pocket protector.

Our young "hero" could have his pick of jobs, own a nice house in the suburbs, but instead Clark Mettles had decided to use his varied talents to counterfeit United States currency.

Ah, youth.

Gage shook his head in disgust, even as he raised his index finger to signal the kid.

Briefcase in hand, Mettles made a beeline for the bar stool next to Gage.

"M-Mr. Angelini?"

Sighing inwardly at the tremble in the kid's voice, Gage tapped the bar. "Drink?"

"Uh—" his gaze darted to Gage's glass "—whatever you're having."

Great. Now the kid would cough all through the meeting.

Gage gave the bartender the order, knowing his cover—Italian-mob-type Gage Angelini—would never talk a fellow criminal into a light beer.

With his dark coloring, it was easy to slip from his native French Creole, to Italian, Black Irish or Hispanic. Different clothes, accents, hairpieces, colored contacts, and presto, a spy is born.

"I brought samples," Mettles said, reaching into his briefcase.

"Not here," Gage said through his teeth.

The documents disappeared into the case.

Though Gage would have been thrilled to get the counterfeit plates and sample bills, hand over the payment and slap on the cuffs, he knew the kid was just a middleman. Mettles didn't put a deal this slick together.

Gage wanted the kid's boss—Joseph Stephano, if the undercover research was accurate. The Treasury Department had been after him for fifteen years, the FBI even longer.

The bartender delivered the drink, and Mettles threw back a healthy gulp, then gasped and coughed for a full minute before choking out, "Water."

Gage ordered water and another drink for himself. It was going to be a long afternoon.

2

"IS MY WIG CROOKED?"

As she unlatched her seat belt, Roxanne eyed Toni's sleek, shoulder-length white-blond hair. Her best friend looked like a cross between the part they planned to play—rich tourists on the make—and a jaded rock star.

Maybe it was the star-shaped crystal glued next to her right eye that sent the disguise over the top.

Roxanne tugged a lock on one side. "It looks great."

Toni angled her head as she stared at herself in the mirror on the car's visor. "I like the shade," she said, fluffing her bangs. "Maybe I'll go lighter with my color next time at the salon."

"It flatters you." Turning the rearview mirror, Roxanne examined her own disguise one last time. She should have known Toni would get carried away with this incognito business.

Her own father wouldn't know her.

A nearly waist-length, ringlet-curled black wig covered her shoulder-length, dark red hair. She wore heavy pancake makeup; smoky eye shadow and black liner rimmed her eyes, which colored contacts had changed from golden-brown to green. Tanning cream and bronzing powder had turned her pale skin a dusky gold. Dark red lipstick gave her lips a sexy pout, and the body-hugging black pantsuit made her curves—enhanced with these weird, gel-like pads in her bra—obvious for anyone to see.

She felt ridiculous.

"I think we should have gone the other way and dressed as cleaning staff," she told Toni.

"No way am I wearing those horrible orthopedic shoes."

"We look *obvious*."

Toni grinned as she applied bright pink lipstick. "Maybe we'll get lucky."

"As long as we don't get caught."

Toni dropped the lipstick in her bag. "Chill. The hotels are crawling with tourists. We'll blend right in."

"I can't believe he lied—again." Roxanne glanced again at Gage's Mercedes, parked just one row over.

After spending most of the afternoon on their disguises, they'd driven to the Sheraton and scoped the parking decks for Gage's car. Without success. So, as her heart pounded and her headache worsened, they'd driven around the other hotels' lots. On the third one, they'd found their quarry. At the Bayou Palace.

"Maybe the meeting's at the Palace, and he's staying at the Sheraton," she said.

Toni rolled her eyes. "Oh, *that's* not reaching. And why would he move the car? The hotels are practically across the street from each other."

"I'm just looking for a way I might have misunderstood."

Toni laid her hand on her shoulder. Her eyes softened. "You're in denial."

Roxanne sighed. "Thanks for being here. I couldn't do this without you."

"We could just have my cousin tow the car and dump it in Lake Pontchartrain."

Though the visual aspects of that plan appealed to her—as well as the idea of turning Gage into a Greta—she discovered she had some of the Lewis resolve after all. "No. I have to see this through."

Toni smiled weakly. "Just think of the adventure we'll have. We haven't gone incognito since we snuck into fraternity parties in college."

"And found your boyfriend snuggling up to a Chi O."

Toni winced. "Right."

The image of Gage and a svelte blonde—not unlike her friend's current look—darted through her mind. She could picture him nuzzling her neck—God, he was a great nuzzler—and whispering naughty suggestions in her ear as she tossed back her head and laughed.

"Hey. Stop thinking about it," Toni said as if she'd read her thoughts. "I've got two gallons of Ben and Jerry's Cherry Garcia stashed in the freezer just in case."

For a moment, Roxanne managed to forget her heartache. "Cherries? I'm gonna need chocolate."

"You're allergic."

"A few coughs aren't going to stop me tonight."

"Fine." Toni shimmied her shoulders. "Until then...let's party." She stepped from the car and tugged her trim pink suit into place, her gold bracelets jangling. "Okay, Foxy Roxy, lead on."

Roxanne ground to a halt. "Damn. We need fake names."

Toni clapped her hands. "Great. I get to be Brandy."

"That sounds like a stripper."

Toni sniffed. "I like it."

"What about me?"

Toni eyed her up and down. "Something exotic, Mediterranean. Marina?"

"Fine."

They wound through the parking garage before getting on an elevator. Roxanne's heart hammered in her chest like a freight train. What would she do if she saw him? What if she found him sitting in the bar draped around another woman? Would she break into tears and run? Slap his face?

Maybe there was a logical explanation for deceiving her. Maybe he'd just gotten the hotels confused. Possible, but depressingly unlikely. Gage was way too careful.

The walk from the parking deck to the lobby seemed to take an eternity, but finally they pushed through the revolving glass door. They walked out, Toni swinging her hips so hard a bellhop tripped into his luggage cart.

Roxanne poked her in the side. "Will you stop? We're supposed to be incognito."

"We're hiding in plain sight."

"This is a mistake," Roxanne said, her stomach suddenly bottoming out.

Toni grabbed her arm and tugged her toward a table of house phones. "You'll hate me tomorrow if I let you back down." She picked up the receiver and handed it to Roxanne. "Besides, it's kind of exciting."

"What do I do with this?"

"Ask the operator to ring Gage's room, of course."

"May I help you?" a voice said through the phone.

"Gage Dabon's room, please."

"I'm sorry. There's no listing under that name."

"What about First National Bank?"

"No, ma'am."

Great. She could feel anger and dread stir deep inside. His car was here, but no room in his name? Maybe the room was registered in his roommate's name. Damn. She should have questioned Gage further.

"I don't suppose you have a John Smith?" Roxanne asked dryly.

"Seventy-two of them."

"Of course. Thanks anyway." Roxanne hung up. "Strike one."

Toni smiled and looked around the opulent, bustling lobby. "Good."

"Good?"

She pulled Roxanne by the wrist. "Now we can troll the bars."

"The next time you get an idea this stupid, remind me to talk you out of it."

Toni laughed, dragging her into the bustling lobby bar. Happy hour was in full swing, without a vacant seat in sight. As they craned their necks and wound through the tables, a pair of young businessmen gallantly gave up their stools at the bar. The men bought them drinks—a Long Island iced tea for Toni and a glass of white wine for Roxanne—and while Toni carried the small talk, Roxanne looked for Gage.

She flinched as each dark-haired man turned around. She strained for the sound of his voice. And frantic explanations scrolled through her mind. The parking deck at the Sheraton was full, so Gage had parked here. The meeting location had changed at the last minute. Gage was meeting a client here, then going to the Sheraton later.

But as much as she wanted to believe these excuses, her sense of practicality doubted it, and her imagination kicked into high gear. Hadn't Gage been distant lately? Distracted? When he'd visited New York two weeks ago, had he really been here? And this week, had he gone to Chicago and come back early? Had he gone at all?

Could he really be cheating on her?

Though she'd never once considered him dishonest, she'd always sensed a dangerous, dark side in Gage. Ironically—given her vow to steer clear of cops—she wondered if that quality had attracted her.

After thirty minutes with no sign of Gage, and with nervous panic fluttering in her belly, she nudged Toni. "Let's go."

Toni batted her lashes in Jr. Executive #1's direction. "In a minute."

She stood and nudged Toni hard enough that her drink sloshed to the rim.

"Oh, right." Toni downed one last slug of *tea*. How the girl drank that stuff and still walked—especially on high-heeled slingbacks—Roxanne had no idea. "Gotta cruise, guys," she said to the suits as she slid off her stool. "Maybe we'll catch you later in the Quarter."

Roxanne nudged her friend. "Let's go, *Brandy*."

Toni's eyes narrowed briefly, then she led the way out of the bar and across the lobby. From a bellhop, they learned there was a quiet piano bar on the twenty-sixth floor, so they headed up.

"I could get into this undercover work," Toni said, inspecting her face in a compact.

Roxanne watched the elevator numbers light in sequence. "We'll sign you up for P.I. school ASAP."

The doors opened, and Toni strode out, Roxanne hot on her heels. The maître d' stand was positioned at the bar's entrance.

How did one go about these things? Following someone, tracking them down, confronting them? She swallowed hard. Why hadn't she paid more attention to her siblings and father when they'd yammered on about their cases?

Tamping down her nerves and regrets, she watched Toni smoothly tell the tuxedo-clad maître d' that she and her companion would prefer to sit in the back. He escorted them across the room to a small table next to the floor-to-ceiling windows, affording them an incredible view of the Mississippi River. Nauseous, Roxanne couldn't appreciate the sight.

A waiter in black pants, white tuxedo shirt and black vest took their orders—Diet Coke for Roxanne and another Long Island iced tea for Toni—and Roxanne decided she would definitely drive home. She fiddled with the drink-special menu, then the gold-rimmed, crystal ashtray, while taking surreptitious glances around the room. It wasn't until the smiling young waiter set her Coke in front of her, then met her gaze directly, frank male appreciation reflected in his eyes, that she remembered her disguise. She was Marina—exotic Mediterranean beauty. The description was so far from the usual her—quiet, ordinary Roxanne—she nearly giggled.

Good grief, she was getting hysterical.

The waiter left, and Roxanne concentrated on scanning the room—the dark, elegant attire of the customers, the quiet conversations, the muted lighting, the quiet strains of the piano.

"He'd like this."

"A bit stuffy for me," Toni said, wrinkling her nose.

Roxanne cast a sideways glance at her friend, wondering, incredulously, when this had become a girls' night out.

"Uh, right." Toni cleared her throat. "Gage."

"He's the reason we're here."

"Of course." Craning her neck, Toni deduced, "He's not here."

"I'm beginning to agree."

Roxanne studied each customer in turn. Though the bar boasted several dark-haired men in conservative suits, none of them were Gage. None had his stark masculinity, his controlled coolness, his sexy—

Whoa. What's this?

A man at one end of the bar had turned. He lifted a dark amber drink to his lips. Sparkles of gold and diamonds winked at his wrist. Broad shoulders filled a black suit jacket. His manner was smooth, confident. Unsmiling, he nodded at his young male companion.

Gage.

Her heart hammered; her mouth went dry. Her gaze locked on his sculpted cheekbones and strong jaw. "He's there," Roxanne said to Toni, even more certain as she said the words aloud.

Toni's head bobbed. "Where?"

"The left side of the bar."

"He's too young."

"The one next to him."

"He's got a—"

"Ponytail, I know."

"He's *smoking*."

Roxanne had noticed that, too. Her whole body grew numb. Her heart sank. "I was kind of expecting a svelte blond lover," Toni said.

"Let's hope it's not the kid sitting next to him."

Toni pursed her lips. "No way."

"That was a joke." Roxanne watched Gage drum his fingers on the bar. He scowled and shook his head, his ponytail sliding against the collar of his jacket. The sophisticated surface she saw every day had been wiped away, replaced by a dark seediness she'd never before associated with Gage. As if the charming man she knew, the man she lived with, was an act, and this dangerous stranger had risen to take his place.

No woman, but a disguise? Tangled emotions assaulted her—relief, confusion, worry, anger. What the hell was going on?

She'd heard of people having a nervous breakdown. She'd heard from her family many times about crimes of passion, people snapped and hurt the ones closest to them. She'd heard on talk shows about defining moments in a person's life.

So in that moment of watching Gage frown at the man next to him, of watching her fiancé act like someone else, appear as someone else...something inside her shifted. Changed.

Snapped.

GAGE GLARED at his young, would-be counterfeiter. "So where is he, Mettles?"

Mettles swallowed, his protruding Adam's apple

shaking. "He said he'd be here." He glanced around. "But he didn't sound pleased."

Gage bit back a nasty remark about waiting for this kid to find his balls. It wouldn't help to lose his cool. He needed all his nerves to confront Stephano. They'd retired to this more private bar on top of the hotel after a cell phone request by Mettles's boss, and though the view of the river and city lights was beautiful, the hairs at Gage's nape twitched.

He turned, expecting to finally come face-to-face with Mettles's boss, but he only saw other patrons, sipping drinks and talking quietly.

Then he saw her.

At a corner table sat a busty, exotic-looking woman with long, curly dark hair. Gage's first impulse was hooker. But as he watched her lift her drink to her deep red lips, he saw a gracefulness and sense of style usually not found in ladies of the night.

A rich tourist trolling for excitement, he amended, though something about the woman and her companion struck him as familiar. Had he seen them before? Maybe they'd been in the lobby bar earlier.

Her blond-haired friend noticed his appraisal and gestured at him. The dark beauty glanced at him, then averted her face, for which Gage was glad. He couldn't afford to attract too much attention. Especially from the type of woman who found the danger emanating from Gage Angelini irresistible.

As nothing seemed to be going right all night, he wasn't surprised to see, out of the corner of his eye, the two women rising. They laid money on the table, then, after a brief discussion, they parted, the blonde heading out of the bar and the exotic beauty heading straight for him.

"Hell." He sipped his drink and waited for her approach. Six months working this stupid case, and it was about to be spoiled by some lonely heart.

Her perfume reached him first. Spicy and mysterious, it stirred him more than he'd anticipated.

"Gage?" she said in a smoky voice.

Startled, Gage's hand jerked. Ice clanged against the crystal.

He turned and met her gaze squarely. Her eyes were a bright emerald green, her skin dark gold, her black jumpsuit filled out with generous curves. He didn't know her, yet something about her was familiar. Was it the shape of her face? Her expression?

Her mouth pursed in irritation. "What are you doing here?"

The itch on the back of his neck intensified, but he somehow remembered his role. He smiled. "Havin' a drink, *bella*. Join me."

Mettles shifted on his stool.

Gage knew what was going through his mind. *My boss isn't going to like this.*

"Move down for the lady, Mettles."

Mettles moved, and Gage took the beauty's hand and assisted her onto the stool. The view of her well-endowed cleavage was impressive, but Gage's brain was too busy spinning a way out of the situation to fully appreciate her body.

"Drink?" he asked her.

She nodded at his glass. "What are you having?"

"Black Jack."

Her gaze flew to his. "You don't—" She stopped and smiled seductively. "That's good for me."

What was with people tonight? This stuff ate away your stomach lining.

He made the order, but continued to stare at the woman. *Something doesn't click. Something's off here.*

For the first time he wondered if he was being set up. Certainly not by Mettles, but maybe Stephano was testing Gage, looking for a trap himself.

Gage pulled his cigarette case from his inside pocket and offered a smoke to the lady.

Her lip curled disdainfully. "No, thanks."

He lit the cigarette and expertly pressed a concealed button on the side of the case as he returned it to his pocket. The case doubled as a camera, and he intended to run his lovely lady's face through the federal criminal database.

He took a drag of the cigarette, fighting the urge to cough. He leaned toward her, speaking so only she could hear. "So, are you going to tell me where I know you from?"

Her full red lips flattened. She practically snarled at him, then she whispered in his ear, "Well, the other night the sex was pretty interesting, even if it was a bit rushed."

Her voice was different this time, less husky. And he knew it. He knew it very well.

Oh, hell.

3

FOR AN INSTANT, Gage's whole body stilled, his heart stopped pumping, his brain froze. Leaning back, he stared at his fiancée. "It can't be," he muttered.

"Oh, but it is." She shoved her chest out and dropped her gaze.

Gage, noting she had much more than usual, stared down. There, between the beautiful breasts he'd nipped and tasted a few nights ago, rested the round sapphire pendant he'd given her for her birthday. His gaze jolted back to hers. "Rox—"

She laid her finger over his lips.

"Angelini."

Gage turned. A tall, slender, silver-haired man—who looked more like a bank executive than a mobster, yet one Gage recognized from surveillance photos—stood at Mettles's quivering side.

Gage pulled Roxanne off her stool and swept her behind him at the same time he gestured to the man. "Mr...?"

His mouth tipped up on one side. "Stephano," he said smoothly as he sat, his cold blue gaze straying to sweep over Roxanne and her formfitting pantsuit.

Gage found it difficult to keep anger out of his voice. "What's your drink?"

"Scotch, neat." He nodded his head at Roxanne. "I

didn't realize we'd arranged a double date. Though Mettles doesn't hold a candle to your lady."

His heart hammering, Gage remembered his role and smiled. "True, but she's more expensive."

The mobster chuckled, and Roxanne gasped in outrage.

"Why, you—" she began.

Gage yanked her arm, so she landed with a plop on the bar stool behind him. He faced her, all but grinding his teeth to stay calm and in control.

Her eyes, normally a comforting shade of brown, spit green fire.

She's in danger. I've put her in danger.

Guilt and fear strengthened his resolve. He glided his hand beneath her jaw and pulled his room card from his pocket with the other. "Go down to my suite, baby. I'll be along later." He brushed his lips against her cheek and whispered, "Please. I can explain. Please go."

Stephano clapped him on the shoulder. "Ah, let her stay. A beautiful woman is always a welcome addition to the party." He smiled lasciviously at Roxanne.

Gage growled low in his throat.

"Don't like sharing, huh, Angelini?" Stephano threw back most of the contents of his drink, his eyes glowing as he stared at Roxanne. "I could make it worth your while."

With every ounce of control and experience he possessed, Gage held his cover. Quickly, he assessed all that had occurred since Roxanne had literally walked into this mess, including his surprise at her appearance, which Mettles had no doubt witnessed. "She can be trouble. She was supposed to stay in the room."

Stephano's eyes gleamed. "I like trouble."

Gage raised one eyebrow, as if he was actually considering the disgusting idea of sharing. "Really?"

Roxanne gasped. She raised her hand—to slap him, Gage presumed, but he caught it and kissed the underside of her wrist. "It'd have to be substantial. She's very good."

Roxanne tried to yank her hand away, but Gage held tight. She could hit him later, though he couldn't imagine Roxanne actually going through with the blow.

Stephano threw back his head and laughed. "Ah, I think we'll work well together, Angelini."

And, just like that, Gage was in.

While Stephano ordered another drink, Gage slid his hand behind Roxanne's head, feeling the edge of the wig she wore. He couldn't help but admire her guts in finding him. He'd known she'd been suspicious of him at lunch, but he'd never dreamed she'd pull something this bold. Remembering her blond companion, he pinned the idea of the disguises on Toni.

And an excellent disguise it was. Fooling him—a ten-year undercover veteran. As if she knew the skills of a pro, she'd altered her appearance significantly, but also latched on to the secret of change—the attitude. Looks alone didn't complete a deception. The transformation had him hard as a rock.

Roxanne always stirred his lust, but this daring, dark beauty was such a contrast from his normally agreeable, elegant fiancée that he found himself even more aroused than usual. Couples had engaged in role-playing games for centuries, he supposed, though he'd never before seen the interest. Now he had a different view. He longed for the moment he could send her anger over into passion, uncovering her body, cementing his hold on her heart.

It would no doubt take all the finesse he had. But he would hold on to her. *She'll know your secret before the night's out. She'll leave you. She'll hate you.*

Maybe. If they lived that long.

He pulled her close, ignoring the panicked racing of his own heart. He'd get her out of there. Safe. Away from the danger and slime he waded in.

Her dusky face turned nearly purple with rage. She wouldn't meet his gaze. "Come on, baby. You know I was just kidding." He brushed a light kiss across her lips. Her mouth remained cold and her lower lip trembled.

Oh, damn, he thought as her eyes filled with tears.

"Hang on," he whispered. "Just play along, Rox. You can do it. Please. We're in big danger here."

She sniffed and offered him a barely perceptible nod. That small measure of trust gave him more hope than he probably deserved. Damn him. He never should have involved her in his risky life.

"How about some champagne, baby?" He snapped his fingers at the bartender. "I've got some business, then I'll take you out."

"Bring the bottle," Stephano ordered the bartender. "Mettles likes the stuff, too." Stephano nudged his employee none too gently. "Right?"

Mettles held on to the bar so he wouldn't fall off the stool. "Yes, sir."

Stephano frowned as the waiter popped the cork, then poured two glasses. "Too sweet for me."

Gage held up his hand. "I'll stick with Black Jack."

Stephano nodded in approval. "Now, *that's* a drink. It'll put hair on your chest, Mettles."

"If you say so, sir."

"Let's toast." Stephano raised his glass. The other three held up their drinks. "To success and rolling in the dough."

"Cheers," they said as one.

Gage watched Roxanne knock back more than half her glass in one swallow. Roxanne rarely drank. She polished off the rest and held out her flute for more. The bartender obliged, and the wheels in Gage's brain churned frantically. This was going to go from bad to worse in a matter of minutes if he didn't get them out of the bar.

But Stephano jumped in. "Mettles, go sit by the lady—" he paused "—hey, Angelini, you never introduced me to your lady."

"This is—"

"Marina." Roxanne's slim arm shot across Gage. She held out her hand, and Stephano kissed the back of it. "Charmed to meet you."

The tears in her eyes had been replaced by a dreamy glaze. *Oh, boy.*

"Lovely." Stephano released her hand. Reluctantly, Gage thought. "Mettles, go entertain the lovely Marina while Gage and I discuss some business."

Mettles leaped off his stool, and they all slid down to make room for him to sit by Roxanne.

Gage had no idea what she would say to an MIT computer-engineering graduate who programmed mob counterfeiting equipment, but Mettles started off by complimenting her outfit. Counterfeiting and fashion, oh *there* was an interesting combination.

"Why don't we meet later for dinner?" he said to Stephano, probably too eagerly, but having Roxanne exposed to these people had every muscle in his body clenched. He couldn't let them touch her. He couldn't let this side of his life compromise his future. She deserved much more.

"To celebrate our deal?" Stephano tapped the rim of his glass, looking suddenly like the shrewd mobster Gage knew him to be. "If there is a deal."

"Of course." Gage had set up his cover very well. He'd check out, and Stephano would let him in. He just needed to get Roxanne away from the sleaze and danger. "But Marina isn't much of a party girl. I'll leave her here."

Stephano gestured behind Gage, and he turned to see Mettles filling Roxanne's glass yet again. "She looks like she's havin' a good time to me."

"Mr. Stephano doesn't like to be disappointed," Mettles put in nervously.

Stephano smiled. "Yeah. Tell Mr. Angelini what happens to guys who disappoint me."

Mettles swallowed, glancing around nervously. "They die," he whispered.

Roxanne knocked over her champagne glass, which

Mettles righted just as quickly. She stared at Gage, her eyes wide with horror.

Stephano, of course, laughed.

"Marina would love to join us for dinner," Gage made himself say, though he had no intention of having Roxanne hang around this investigation. He listened carefully as Stephano turned the conversation back to their deal, his possible percentage, the money he wanted transferred if he decided to let Gage "invest." Gage activated the recorder concealed in his watch, but didn't expect to get much. The gangster was careful to use code words and euphemisms, never saying *money* or *plates*. The key to the investigation was finding the place where everything was being manufactured, tracing the operation to Stephano, so warrants could be issued and arrests made.

Roxanne tossed her head back, a giggle escaping her mouth. Gage fought to focus on Stephano, wondering how quickly they could escape, and fighting an intensified arousal at her laughter. She had a beautiful mouth, soft, full bottom lip, and when she kissed her way to his ear and bit down...

Oh, man. He shifted on his stool, the tightness of his groin growing uncomfortable.

"How soon do we start?" he asked Stephano, desperate to stay focused.

Stephano's cagey smile appeared. "Soon."

Gage thought about his groin. And Roxanne's lips.

They'd never actually met, but Gage had dreamed. Probably more often than he should. But Roxanne was shy, caring and sweet. Encouraging her to...explore him that way always seemed too...wild. But he still thought about it—a lot.

"I've got several deals cooking at the moment," Stephano went on.

Gage fought for professional detachment. Gambling? Drugs? Prostitution? All of it sickened him. At some point, would he become sick with himself? "I'm sure," he said, striving for a bored, jaded tone.

"You know I'm particular about business."

Gage met the man's chilling eyes. "Yes."

"I know you only by reputation."

Gage nodded.

"I'm definitely considering moving on this deal, but don't screw with me." He paused. "As Mettles said, I can be...difficult."

Recognizing the warning, the cold-bloodedness not even vaguely disguised, Gage clenched his glass. His head spun, though not from alcohol. He'd poured most of his drinks with Mettles into a nearby plant. The implications of the last few minutes had rattled his thoughts. His personal life and his professional life had merged. His worst nightmare.

"We'll suit each other," Gage said, then downed the rest of the drink.

Stephano rose. "You and your lady freshen up. We'll meet in the lobby in an hour."

Gage lit a cigarette—his nerves might actually need the tobacco at this point. "Sure."

"We'll celebrate. There's a great Italian restaurant on Chartres Street. We'll take my limo and relax."

Trapped in a dark car with a mobster heading to an

Italian restaurant. Holy hell, when had his life become an episode of *The Sopranos*? "Sure."

Stephano smiled at Roxanne. "I'll see you at dinner, Marina."

Her gaze rose slowly. Gage noted her large, black pupils and the exaggerated way she lifted her hand to pat Stephano's cheek—and swore, internally and viscously.

"Sure, honey," she said, then gulped a swallow of champagne.

Stephano smiled, then kissed the back of her hand. His gaze lingered on Roxanne's longer than necessary. "An hour. Mettles, with me." He strode off.

Fists clenched, Gage stood next to his fiancée—the delicate flower he'd fought so hard to protect. And miserably failed. "Let's go."

She plopped down her champagne flute and slid off the stool. "Sure, Gage, baby. This has been a blast."

She wasn't so tipsy that she couldn't inject a tone of sarcasm into her words. Even as Gage admired her guts, he tossed a few bills on the bar and wondered how he'd ever manage to save the best—really the only—relationship in his life.

SOMEWHERE BETWEEN fuzzy fear and hot rage, Roxanne stood back to let Gage unlock his room. He eased the door open and nodded for her to go in first.

Her gaze bounced around the elegant, sunken living area, noting the bedroom off to the left. Blinking back tears, her gaze latched on to the windows across the suite. She moved toward them, laying her palm against the cool glass, staring at the lights below.

The whole night seemed a dream. Or a nightmare. She couldn't even remember how much time had passed since she'd watched her reflection in the mirror as Toni had transformed her from a pale, plain redhead into an exotic Gypsy.

Toni. At least she'd had the sense—maybe premonition—to send her friend out of the bar. She'd wanted to confront Gage alone.

"I need to call Toni. She's waiting downstairs."

Gage laid his hand on her shoulder. "I'll—"

She shrugged. "Don't touch me."

Silence. Then his hand fell away. His breathing seemed the only sound to fill the room, and she longed to turn and find his gaze. But those eyes had looked into hers and lied too often.

"I'll get you down there," he said. "You can leave."

She nodded. But she had questions first.

She might not like her dad's and siblings' jobs, she might distance herself from anything relating to their work, she might still grieve for the tragic, unnecessary loss of her gentle mother, but she hadn't spent twenty years in the Lewis household wearing blinders.

Gage wearing a disguise. That Stephano character with his dead eyes. She wanted to laugh. Hysterically. Her fears of infidelity seemed so distant. The reality might be much, much worse.

Beneath the dull layer of alcohol, her stomach churned. "Who are you, Gage?" she asked quietly.

He sighed. Then, as she sensed him moving away from her, she turned. He paced alongside the glass and chrome coffee table. His long legs ate up the distance quickly, and even as she wanted to throw something at him, she had to admire his profile—the strong jaw, the broad shoulder, the curve of his tight backside. As long as she lived, she doubted she'd ever find a man she wanted as much. Before tonight, she'd even thought she loved him.

But now betrayal and anger and fear vibrated in her veins. She fought to stay calm. She wanted to give him time to explain. Though how any of this could make sense, she couldn't imagine.

He stopped finally. He stared directly at her. Their gazes locked—brown to green, instead of silver to gold. She wanted to scream at the deception. "Dammit, Gage, what the hell is going on?"

"I'm a cop. A Secret Service agent working undercover for the Enforcement Division of the United States Treasury Department."

Her heart jumped. "Come again?"

He disappeared into the bedroom, then returned moments later, holding out a badge: Gage C. Dabon, U.S. Treasury.

"Secret Service agents protect the president."

"That's only one of our functions. The ATF and the Customs Service fall under the Treasury Department. We also investigate a variety of financial crimes."

Light-headed, knowing it wasn't the champagne, she raised her gaze to his. "What does the 'C' stand for?" She didn't know her own fiancé's middle name. How ridiculous was *that*?

His mouth tipped up on one side. "Colin. After my father. He's my boss." He paused. "He reports directly to the undersecretary of enforcement."

He'd told her his mom and dad had retired to a

planned golf community in Florida. Was anything they'd shared real? Would she ever really know? Did she even care?

Gage is a cop. A *federal* cop. A bark of laughter escaped. Then another. She sank to the floor.

Gage knelt beside her. "You're upset."

"You bet your sweet ass I am."

"And pissed. You've cussed at me twice in the last minute."

"You deserved it."

His eyes flashed—with regret, with other emotions. Deeper feelings? Or was that, too, a lie? "I'm sorry."

She glanced at their joined hands, then back to his face. "I'm not sure I believe you."

He flinched. "It'll never be the same, will it?"

"No," she said slowly, her breath catching in her throat, knowing she'd certainly never be the same. "I don't think it will."

As she concentrated on controlling her breathing, some part of her started to accept the situation. Gage wasn't a banker. He didn't trade stocks or advise on investment strategies. He'd lied to her with every breath he'd taken. That dangerous side she'd sensed was a reality, not a sexual fantasy she'd imagined. Her thoughts in the bar came back to her...*as if the charming man she knew, the man she lived with was an act, and this dangerous stranger had risen to take his place.*

That was the reality. She drew a breath, then let the air seep. As she rose to her feet, his arms slid around her, and the tension in the room suddenly changed. She remembered way too many nights of whispered passion and shared need. One controlled stroke of his fingers could bring her completion like she'd never known before. Rolling waves of fulfillment, a gasp of surprise. Her stomach clenched at the thought. Warmth sparked between her legs, then spread outward. With him moving inside her, she'd felt powerful, invulnerable.

She wanted that feeling again.

But her world had spun completely around, and he'd caused the pain. No matter how she longed to touch him, she kept her arms stiff at her sides.

"I'm so sorry I dragged you into this, Rox."

"I'm sure."

His hands roamed her back. "Surely you understand why I couldn't tell you."

She stepped back. "I don't." Then, she added, "I understand why you didn't at first, but not after we got...close." *Intimate. Supposedly in love.* "But not later. We were supposed to be married, Gage."

He went very still. *"Were?"*

She'd already put their relationship in the past, she realized. In an effort to convince him? Or herself?

But she wasn't going there. Too many other problems and questions and lies lay between them. "What about Mettles and Stephano? Who are they?"

"It's a case. I can't really divulge—"

She jabbed her finger in his chest. "Well, you'd better start divulging, buddy. I'm not leaving here until I know what the hell is going on."

He winced. "More cussing?"

She scowled. "I'm in the middle of this mess. Start spilling."

His face turned stony. "No, you're not."

Roxanne wasn't about to debate the point at the moment, but she'd landed herself in a dangerous mess and escape wasn't going to be easy. "You owe me an explanation."

He stared at her silently as the air conditioner clicked on. Finally, he slid his hands into his pockets and said, "I'm investigating a counterfeiting operation. Stephano is the ringleader."

"And Mettles?"

"Clark Mettles is the brains."

"You're kidding."

"An MIT-educated engineer who thinks crime *does* pay."

Disgusted, Roxanne shook her head. "Kids today."

"We think alike, babe."

She stiffened. They were so little alike, she wanted to cry.

He crossed to the black, marble-topped bar, then poured himself a drink. "You want something?"

She rubbed her temples. "No. Yes. Coffee." Sinking onto the sofa, she sighed and wondered if the caffeine would help her get her thoughts in order or just make her jumpy and irritable. "And Gage Angelini?"

"A less than honest, but wealthy businessman willing to invest in the project for a cut of the profits." He started the coffee, then crossed the room, sitting on the table in front of her. "Is my cover worse than finding out I'm a cop?"

She stared down at her hands, linking her fingers to stop the shaking, then glanced up to find his serious gaze on her face. She'd shared her negative views about loved ones in law enforcement many times. She may have even said she'd never date a cop. "I'm not sure," she said finally.

He rolled his crystal glass between his hands and said nothing.

From the angle of his body, with his head bowed, his ponytail caught her attention. Truthfully—and God knew she needed a bit of truth at the moment—it fascinated her. Discovering that dark side truly existed, and probably defined the real him, was enticing, tempting her far more than it should.

He lied to you, her conscious reminded her. *He's made a fool of you. He doesn't care about you. He's using you....* Though for what she couldn't imagine.

She shook away these thoughts and concentrated on the ponytail. It had to be fake, of course. Gage's hair was trimmed conservatively whenever she saw him. She found herself wondering how he'd attached the ponytail and longed to thread her fingers through the black, silky-looking strands. She lifted her hand to—

"It's an extension."

She jerked her hand back, embarrassed he'd caught her staring and that she'd nearly touched him. This man was a stranger. He'd lied. He'd *proposed.* Then he'd lied some more. None of this was real. Nothing about him was real.

"What?" she asked, as if she didn't know he'd responded to her unspoken curiosity.

"The ponytail. It's a hair piece woven into the back of my hair." He set his glass aside, then wrapped a long, curly strand of her black hair around his finger. "A wig, I guess."

"Of course. You're wearing dark brown contacts."

He nodded. "And green for you. Toni's idea, I assume."

"Her shop came in handy."

"You sensed something today at lunch."

She pressed her lips together for a second. She should have known she wasn't fooling him. "She saw you in the Quarter last night. This case, I guess."

"What are the odds?" He shook his head, as if the path they'd traveled to get here was irrelevant. And, in a weird way, it was. "I was arranging with a minor player to meet Mettles," he continued as his hand slid to cup her face, his eyes darkened with tenderness. "I'm so sorry. I never wanted to hurt you."

He had. She knew it. He knew it. It seemed ridiculous to deny her feelings.

He rubbed the pad of his thumb across her cheekbone, sending sparks shooting down her body, even as she longed for the strength to pull away. "The dusky makeup really completes the look." His eyes turned dark, smoky. A look of desire she recognized all too well. "If I didn't know you..."

What? she wanted to ask. What would you do with me? *To* me? Even as an illicit thrill raced through her at the idea of actually being able to pick up Gage at a bar, take him back to her hotel room and explore his body well into the night, she wondered if a woman that confident would have accepted and been fooled by his lies.

"Tanning cream and bronzing powder," she said.

His gaze slid down her body, lingering on the

plunging neckline. "You two looked like tourists on the make."

Surprising pleasure rushed through her, and she remembered those first few moments after she'd approached him. He'd had no idea who she was. Gage Dabon, savvy, hardened—he'd always seemed hardened, even as a banker—experienced Secret Service agent fooled by Roxanne the quiet accountant. "We certainly convinced you."

"You did," he admitted, though he seemed reluctant. "The attitude sent the disguise over the top. You were bold."

She *had* kind of gone full force with the Mysterious Mediterranean Marina thing. "Really?"

His thumb, stroking her face, brushed her earlobe. His white teeth flashed in a knowing smile. Even with the slick ponytail and brown eyes—maybe even *because* of them—he made her libido hum a merry tune. "Mmm. Bold and adventurous."

Hunger rolled off him. He wanted her. Really. Now. The fact that she could want him so much in return should have worried her. Instead, she felt strong. "You liked it?"

His hot breath brushed her cheek. "Very much."

"Was I sexy?"

"Oh, yeah." He leaned forward, his lips a breath from hers. "Totally unlike yourself."

As his warm, persuasive mouth settled on hers, she desperately wanted to sink into him, forget the circumstances that had brought them to this place, indulge in unrelenting, overwhelming passion. She recalled his gentle, then sometimes demanding, touch.

The waves of satisfaction he alone could bring. But his words seeped into her brain.

Sexy... Totally unlike yourself.

She planted her hand on his shoulder and shoved. Hard. "I don't think so," she said confidently, rising.

Maybe it was the "Marina" disguise, maybe she'd tapped into some hidden inner strength, or maybe she was just completely pissed off, but she found the assurance to move away from him. A month ago, a week ago, hell, an hour ago, she would have let him pull her under the spell of passion. But not now. Maybe not— she drew a deep breath—ever.

The trust she'd had in him had been shattered tonight. And she'd never let him break her heart again. No matter what else happened, he was a cop. She'd held up her part in the deception earlier, but the moment they were safe...bye, bye, baby.

"I thought you were cheating on me," she said, facing him, her arms crossed over her chest.

Gage clenched his jaw. How could she think—

He stopped himself. She'd thought a great deal about him tonight—and none of it good. "I'm not— I wouldn't—" Damn, given his deception, no response sounded right. And he feared nothing in his life would ever seem right again. Still reeling from her rejection of his touch, his brain buzzed with plans to bind her to him, even as another part of him scrambled to find a way to save his investigation. *We were supposed to be married.*

They *would* be married.

And he *would* get Stephano.

"I'm not that kind of man?" she asked in a mocking

tone he'd never envisioned her thinking, much less voicing. "I wouldn't cheat on you? I wouldn't *lie* to you?"

As she spun away, he took a step toward her. "Roxanne, I—" Didn't mean to lie to you? To hurt you? He'd known he was doing those things and did them anyway. Denying his actions seemed petty and worthless. The coffee hissed into the pot, punctuating the silence with monotony. "I'll get the coffee."

He retrieved a steaming cup, adding cream and sugar as she liked, all the while rolling plans around his brain. He had to get her out of the hotel undetected. And she had to be long gone before the meeting with Stephano. He wouldn't let that oily mobster get his grimy hands on Roxanne. Somehow, he'd finesse his way through the man's anger at being denied her presence.

Oh, yeah, then he had to save the only relationship he gave a damn about.

You can do all that in your sleep, Gage.

Right.

As he carried coffee to Roxanne, he prioritized his plans—first, her safety, then Stephano, then relationship. He handed her the mug. "We need to get all that off you."

Sipping her coffee, she lifted her eyebrows. "Think again."

No sex. He fought a wince over that bit of reality. Roxanne had never refused him, but at the moment her safety was a priority. He had to stop acting like a man and start acting like a cop. "I meant the costume." He retrieved shorts and a shirt from the bedroom. "Put these on. If any of Stephano's goons spot us, they won't recognize you."

She nodded and started toward the bedroom. Then she stopped. "What will Stephano do when I don't show up in the lobby?"

Gage shrugged, though the volatile mobster wasn't exactly known for his graciousness. It was rumored he'd once cut off an associate's thumb with a switchblade for bringing Stephano the wrong brand of scotch. "He'll get over it."

"Come on, Gage. He's not going to just say, 'Gee, that's too bad,' when you tell him I'm not coming to dinner. You heard Mettles. He'll kill you."

"I'll tell him we had a fight and you ran out on me."

She frowned. "Won't that look like you can't control me?"

"I don't want to control you."

She sighed and walked toward him.

The woman certainly had some kind of walk in that cat suit. Sweat popped out on his forehead.

"I know you don't want to control *me* me, but you want the mob to think you can control Marina me. It's a loss-of-manly-respect thing." She angled her head. "Are you sure you've done this before?"

Irritated, he snapped, "Of course I've done this before. How do you know about the mob and their codes?"

"I've lived with cops all my life. You tend to absorb some of that stuff between *pass the potatoes* at the dinner table."

Who *was* this creature? Certainly not *his* Roxanne. Shy, sweet Roxanne who blushed prettily when he whispered sexual suggestions in her ear and liked to attend the ballet and symphony. His Roxanne didn't calmly discuss the intricacies of mob retaliations.

But as he looked at her ultralong, dark hair, dusky skin and the determination shining out of her green eyes, he reminded himself nothing would ever be the same after tonight. "It'll be fine. I'll work it out."

Concern crossed her face. "What if you don't?" She paused. "Or can't?"

"Worried about me, Rox?"

She said nothing for a moment, and, ridiculously, Gage found himself wanting her to throw her arms around him and sob against his chest. He wanted her to be worried. He wanted so very much for her to truly care. Would that weakness get them killed?

"Yes," she whispered. "I think I am."

With the pad of his thumb, he stroked her check. Tenderness and regret flowed through him. "I'm honored."

Her eyes flashed. "I should just leave you to Stephano's wrath." Her gaze roved his face—no doubt looking for the man she'd spent the last six months with, a man who didn't exist.

We were supposed to be married. He desperately wanted to ask where they stood, but felt selfish asking. He'd find a way to hold on to her. He *had* to.

"But I can't." She tossed his clothes on the table and gulped coffee. "I stumbled into this case, putting you in jeopardy. I won't leave you to deal with the consequences."

After all he'd done to her she was willing to help

him? His heart hammered. "Go home," he said quickly, before he could ask her to stay.

She shook her head. "He'll kill you."

While Stephano might certainly want to, or even try to, bigger and badder guys than him had found out the hard way that Gage Dabon wasn't ready to meet St. Peter. "There's nothing for you to do."

"He expects me there."

"He'll get over it."

She stamped her foot. "Why are you being so stubborn? You need me."

He did, but not professionally. He couldn't allow her to risk herself—not for him and certainly not for Stephano—so he made his words sharp. "I don't."

The Roxanne he knew would have bowed her head and turned away, hurt but not argumentative. This Roxanne—rather like much of the night—didn't act as expected. "Yes, you do. Stephano will let his guard down around a woman. I can distract him."

Gage knew for certain Roxanne didn't want the kind of attention Stephano would offer. He didn't just want to smile and hold her hand. And Gage would strangle the murdering creep on the spot before he'd let him touch her. "No."

"I want to help."

"An experienced undercover cop could handle this, but not you."

She set her coffee mug on the table with a bang. "Damn you, Gage."

She could damn him all she wanted, but she'd be safe. He grabbed her arm. "Let's go." Glancing at her head, he yanked off her wig.

She tried to jerk away from him. "Ow!" She rubbed her hairline. "That was attached with bobby pins, you know."

"Sorry." He tossed the wig on the sofa. Seeing Roxanne's naturally red hair pinned into a bun at the nape of her neck made him feel more balanced. *His* Roxanne was under there after all. The stress of the night had obviously disturbed her greatly. That was the reason she'd impulsively offered to help. She didn't really want anything to do with intrigue and danger. She'd told him so dozens of times.

"No matter what's between us, I won't let them kill you." She tried to wrench her arm from his grasp. "Dammit, Gage, I understand more than anybody about revenge. I'm not leaving."

Her mother.

Hell. He empathized with her pain, but he couldn't let her risk her life. The very idea was wild and irresponsible. Points that defined him professionally, but he couldn't risk Roxanne. She meant too much.

He dragged her to the door. "Sure you are."

"We're meeting Stephano in the lobby in—" she glanced at her watch "—thirty-five minutes. But, hey, if you're not around, I'm sure I can find the mob on my own. Are citizen's arrests really valid?"

Gage halted, glaring at her. "Damn you, Roxanne."

She smiled. "I thought you'd agree."

4

ROXANNE TUGGED the neckline of her pantsuit. If she leaned over more than an inch—

"Stop fidgeting," Gage said sharply, his gaze pinned on the closed elevator doors. "You're the kind of woman who *wants* every man within a mile staring at her chest."

She glared at him. "I know how to act. I fooled you earlier, remember?"

A muscle along his jaw twitched.

"Nobody's watching now. I can adjust if I want."

His gaze flicked to the upper left corner of the elevator. "Nobody except the hotel security guard and whoever else happens to be wandering around his office." He stared at her, his eyes dark, serious and worried. "Never let go of your cover. Someone is always watching."

She rolled her shoulders. Maybe he had a point. She really wished she had Toni with her for support and advice, but she'd called her friend and told her to go home, that she and Gage were trying to work things out together. *One more lie on top of all the others.*

"Fine," she snapped, avoiding Gage's penetrating gaze to watch the floor numbers light in succession.

It was going to be a long night, she decided. Ever since she'd forced Gage into accepting her help—or else risk his precious case—they'd snapped and barked at each other like a couple of dogs after the same bone.

She was surprised by how much Gage's lack of confidence in her hurt. Of course, she wasn't trained for this kind of work, and she didn't have any experience, and his life as well as hers hung in the balance of her actions, and—

Frowning, she realized why he was so worried. How *was* she going to pull this off? *Why* was she even trying?

She was an *accountant*. Exactly when had she become delusional enough to think she could imitate Mata Hari?

Before she had time to dwell on her regrets, the elevator stopped and the doors slid open.

Gage laid his hand at the small of her back and urged her forward, and her heart leaped to her throat. "You're doing fine," he whispered close to her ear.

Ridiculously, she was comforted by his presence. She might never trust Gage the man again, but she knew instinctively she could at least count on the cop.

She nodded and forced a smile to her lips. She swung her hips as she walked, and pretended a confidence she didn't feel. Roxanne might be an accountant, but Marina was a babe.

"That's some kind of walk you've got, Marina," Gage whispered, his voice low and seductive.

Roxanne's stomach fluttered, and her confidence rose. She could do this.

Babe, babe, babe... she repeated to herself as her high-heeled pumps clacked against the lobby's marble floor. She kept her head high and concentrated on her hip-swaying, letting Gage guide her around a group of chattering tourists. She was so focused she didn't see the impending disaster until it literally jumped out at her.

Actually, until *she* jumped out.

Toni, that is. From behind one of the potted palms scattered around the lobby.

"Hey," she said, grabbing Roxanne's arm and tugging her behind the plant.

Glancing around frantically, Roxanne shook off her friend's grip. "I thought I told you to go home."

Blue eyes narrowed, Toni shook her head. Her blond, bobbed wig swung. "I'm not leaving you here with *him*."

She loved the stubborn woman, she really did, but now was not the time to tangle with Toni's innate determination.

Gage leaned toward Toni. "We're working this out. We need some time alone."

"So Roxanne said on the phone." Toni crossed her arms over her chest. "Unconvincingly, I might add."

As much as she appreciated Toni's protection, Roxanne silently swore. She shifted her gaze across the lobby, trying to inconspicuously spot Stephano and Mettles. If they saw Toni...

She shivered. Finding herself in the middle of a mob sting was dangerous and surreal enough. Putting Toni in danger as well wasn't a development she wanted to consider.

"Go away, Toni," Gage said, his gaze hard.

Roxanne jabbed him with her elbow. "Don't challenge her, for heaven's sake." She grabbed her friend's hands. "Toni, I'm fine." When she continued to glare,

Roxanne added, "I'm safe with Gage. We have some...issues to work out."

"*Blond* issues?"

Her suspicions of infidelity. Damn. Even if she told Toni her fears had turned out to be unfounded, her friend would still wonder. She'd wonder if Gage had managed to snow her. Toni had been with her too many times when Roxanne had been so snowed they'd needed a plow to dig her out. She had to find a way to convince Toni there was a logical explanation for Gage with a ponytail, who'd been caught in too many lies.

"Gage's auditioning for a play," she blurted out.

Toni rolled her eyes. "Oh, please."

Roxanne nodded frantically, even as Gage sighed. "Yep. Monday morning. So we only have a few days to work out the kinks in his performance." She patted Toni's shoulder. "You just go on home, and I'll—"

"What's he playing?" Toni asked.

"Uh...well...uh—" She glanced at Gage, then back at Toni. "An artist. Yep. An eccentric artist. Sort of an Italian Van Gogh thing."

"And what's this play called?"

"*The Ponytail That Roared,*" Roxanne returned without missing a beat.

Toni rolled her eyes again. "*Please.*"

"I'm okay. Really. I need you to go home. I'll give you an update after the weekend."

Toni opened her mouth—no doubt to argue—then just as abruptly closed it. Her sharp blue gaze penetrated Roxanne's until Roxanne wanted to flinch, but she didn't, sensing her friend needed to see she was okay. "I don't know what you two are up to," she said finally, "and I don't think I like it one bit, but at least he's not holding you hostage."

Roxanne blinked. "Hostage? He wouldn't—"

After tonight she supposed she couldn't begin a sentence concerning Gage with "he wouldn't." His lies and disguise, his being a cop, her being involved in a mob sting. Regardless, she was beyond being able to explain from behind the potted palm in the lobby of the Bayou Palace while she and Gage waited for a mob boss and his MIT-educated counterfeiting expert to arrive for dinner.

"I'll call you Monday," she said firmly to Toni.

Toni's gaze slid to Gage. Suspicion flashed through her eyes, but she hugged Roxanne, then stepped back. "Before ten, or I'm calling the Cavalry."

In other words, her family. Damn. She'd better inform her dad of her plans. If he happened to phone her house, and she didn't return his call, he'd have half the NOPD looking for her.

"Before ten," she promised. She watched Toni walk away, trim hips swaying in her tight pink suit.

"At least now I know who taught you that walk," Gage said from behind her.

Roxanne elbowed him in the stomach.

TEN MINUTES LATER, she sat in the lobby bar, pretending to sip champagne.

Beside her, Gage scanned the room while appearing to simply enjoy her company.

The act, naturally, had Roxanne zipping through her memories, searching other nights and other "dates" for falsehoods and inconsistencies. Would it always be like this? Would she always wonder where he was? Where he'd been?

She shook her head. No. It wouldn't *always* be anything. After this weekend, her relationship with Gage was over. O-V-E-R. She wanted nothing to do with his lifestyle. The lies. The danger. She wanted a family someday. A normal house. Children. She didn't want to worry about her husband carrying a gun, playing games of intrigue with criminals, on a stakeout, testifying against society's worst.

Yet, at the same time, her heart hammered with an odd kind of excitement. Had balancing accounts ever caused this kind of nervous, yet electrifying, anticipation?

Uh, no.

Numbers are safe, numbers are safe, she repeated silently to herself, squashing the idea that she might actually be enjoying the espionage. She reached into her purse for her cell phone and began dialing her father's house.

Gage's hand covered hers. "Who are you calling?"

"None of your business," she retorted, crossing her legs and holding the phone to her ear.

Gage simply pulled the phone from her grasp. But before she could do more than gasp at his arrogance, he'd glanced at the digital screen and handed it back. "Keep it brief."

She jerked the phone to her ear just in time to hear her dad's commanding voice say "...leave a message at the tone." After the obligatory beep, Roxanne told the machine that she and Gage had decided to get away for the weekend, and if her dad needed to get in touch with her, he should call her cell phone.

The moment she concluded the call, Gage lifted his crystal tumbler from the bar. With the glass against his lips, he commented, "Nicely done. Now turn off the phone. I don't want it ringing during dinner."

Though seeing the sense in his advice, Roxanne glared at him. What had ever possessed her to feel obligated to save his miserable hide? He was domineering, arrogant, high-handed, dangerous...

Tender, loving...*lonely*.

She sighed and did as he'd asked. She wasn't likely to resolve her feelings for Gage in a night. Maybe not even in a lifetime.

She took a tiny sip of champagne. Though she felt sober as a nun, she knew from her cop family that sobriety was an illusive concept. She needed to pace herself with Stephano and his hard-partying crowd. "Where are they?"

Gage obviously didn't need an explanation of *they*. "Stalling. Purposely." He laid his forearms casually against the bar, while she leaned her back against the polished wood and faced the tables scattered around the drinking and lounging area. She wondered about the positioning but didn't ask. Maybe this way, with Gage's back to the room, was his idea of showing these people he trusted them, which he most certainly didn't.

"It's a power thing," he continued. "They want *me* waiting on *them*." He shrugged his broad shoulders—and Roxanne convinced herself she didn't remember their breadth and muscle *at all*. "It's part of the game I can live with. Though it is somewhat high school. Like pretending to be cool so you can belong to the popular crowd."

"Gage, you don't have to pretend to be cool."

His smile flashed, quick and unexpected.

The sight of those straight white teeth put Roxanne's libido on edge. How weird was *that*?

"I think that was a compliment."

"Don't get used to it."

"Still pissed?"

"Immensely."

"I guess that means sex is out the question."

Despite the seriousness—and, she had to admit, the temptation of his offer—Roxanne had to bite back a smile. "Way out."

Then she saw them. Stephano and Mettles strolled out of the elevators, with the computer engineer scuffling at his boss's heels. Stephano held his head high, his posture proud and erect. His silver hair glinted off the chandeliers. He looked for all the world like a successful businessman, comfortable with his posh surroundings. Roxanne wondered how many people realized his aura of wealth and power came at the expense of others' suffering.

"They're here," Gage said quietly.

Roxanne stared at him. "How did you—"

"You've got a hell of a grip, Marina."

Roxanne glanced at her hand, which was currently squeezing the life out of Gage's bicep. She let go and fought to calm her racing heart. "Sorry."

"You'll be fine. Just smile a lot and say as little as possible."

"Gee, Gage, how will I *ever* manage that? I'd *so* looked forward to discussing trends in computer engineering with Mr. Mettles."

"Your tongue is unusually sharp tonight, my dear."

"It's either that or I fall to the floor in terrified hysterics."

He slid his strong, warm hand over hers, lifting her wrist to his lips. "I'll take the tongue any day."

Pulse zipping, Roxanne stared at him. Even with dark brown eyes, the intensity in his expression did amazing things to her pulse. In a way, she wished she could rewind to when she'd been blissfully unaware of Gage's other life, when she'd spent every moment with him basking in his attention and the desire they shared. She wanted his touch again so desperately she nearly asked him to hold her, but her conscience, thankfully, prodded and nagged and reminded her why that would be a really lousy idea at the moment.

"Angelini and the lovely Miss Marina," Stephano said. His tone pushed for charm, but somehow still managed to sound oily.

While Roxanne smiled wanly, Gage laid a twenty on the bar and rose. "Ready?"

Stephano extended his arm. "My limo's out front." His icy blue gaze dropped briefly to Roxanne's cleavage as she stood.

Resisting the urge to cringe, Roxanne shamelessly clung to Gage as they walked from the bar and out the lobby doors. The ever-present humidity hit her face like a damp blanket, and sweat immediately popped out between her breasts. The temperature, along with the sight of the shiny but ominous-looking black stretch limo parked at the curb, caused a sick roll through her stomach.

Gage kept his hand on her waist as they ducked inside the plush interior. His presence brought her some comfort, though she wasn't sure what he could do if

Stephano decided they were expendable and chose to shoot them, then dump their bodies in Lake Pontchartrain.

Would asking to check the trunk for cement be too obvious?

As the limo pulled away, Stephano prepared himself, then Gage, yet another drink. These two were going to be out on the floor in a minute.

He and Gage launched into a conversation about the stock market, while Roxanne turned her head and watched the lights of the city roll by. The hotels, restaurants and shops were familiar. This was her city; the place she'd lived all her life. Yet tonight it seemed distant and stifling. She was trapped in this car, trapped in another life.

"Marina is a lovely name," Clark Mettles said, smiling hesitantly in her direction. "Italian?"

Roxanne shook off her claustrophobic sensations and nodded. "After my grandmother." She did have an Italian grandmother, and Gage had told her to stick to the truth as much as possible when faced with personal questions, as they didn't have the time or resources to create an entire dossier for her. Earlier, he'd confiscated all her credit cards and driver's license, tucking them into a concealed compartment in his briefcase. She'd half expected "Q" to pop out from behind the hotel-room curtains with more James Bondish gadgets and instructions.

"My parents visited Italy last summer. Beautiful country."

"So I've heard. Never had the chance to go myself."

"You should ask Mr. Angelini to take you. I understand he's been many times."

A polite comment? Or a subtle warning that they were tracking Gage's every move? Frankly, cute, but nerdy-looking Clark didn't seem sophisticated enough to pull off a double-edged conversation, but he didn't get his MIT degree by being anybody's dummy either.

"I'll do that," she said to him.

Clark stared out the window for a few moments, then asked, "So how about your parents? Are they Italian, too?"

Obviously, Clark had been assigned the task of chatting up the one unknown in this wild scenario. Her. Sweat rolled down her spine. "My mother was, but my father's Irish."

"Was?"

Her stomach fluttered, as it always did when she thought of the violent death of her gentle mother. "She passed away a number of years ago."

Gage, bless him, was apparently listening to her conversation as well as his own, since he patted her arm. "The precious-metals market is bound to make a comeback. Marina might even personally see to it."

Stephano roared with laughter.

Roxanne flushed, but from that moment on, Stephano and Gage included her in their discussion, and Clark's personal questions stopped. Throughout dinner, though, she was sandwiched in a black leather–covered booth between Gage and Stephano, each determined to outcharm her. Gage stroked her arm. Stephano laid his hand on her knee. Gage stared into her eyes. Stephano ogled. Gage suggested. Stephano implied.

She felt like a meaty bone caught between two bloodhounds. Or maybe a shepherd and a rottweiler.

Stephano ate a two-inch-thick steak and baked potato swimming in butter and sour cream with as much gusto as he downed scotch. Maybe the Treasury Department would get lucky and the guy would drop dead from a heart attack. Save the taxpayers a pile of money. By the time a thick slice of cheesecake appeared in front of each diner, Roxanne could actually feel her arteries hardening, and Gage's jaw had become so rigid she wouldn't have been surprised if it popped.

Jealousy? she wondered.

Ha! her conscience shot back. *He's just afraid you'll sue the department for sexual harassment of a civilian.*

But his eyes were dark and his fingers gentle as they stroked the back of her hand. He seemed genuinely worried—

Genuine? Just which part of "He's lied every moment since you've met" don't you understand?

Oh, shut up.

Just what she needed—a bossy conscience.

Finally, *finally*, Stephano brought up the topic everyone had been quietly holding their breaths for. "So, Angelini, you'd like in on my little project?"

Looking very much in his element, Gage leaned back. "I hear you could use new investors."

"Mmm. I had one fall out recently."

Fall out? Just exactly how—or from what—had he fallen out?

She wanted to grab Gage's hand and run from the restaurant. What was he doing in the middle of this?

Somebody had to fight the bad guys, she supposed, but why did it have to be him?

Why does it have to be you, Daddy? Why can't you own a shoe store like Suzie Mancuso's father?

With effort, she jerked herself from the past and concentrated on Gage's response.

"I have some capital I need to shift. I like aspects of your project, but Mettles has been short on details."

Stephano tossed his napkin on the table. "Naturally. He understands my need for discretion. If you're looking for a company mission statement, Angelini, you're doomed to disappointment."

Gage accepted this warning with a mere angling of his head. The rakish angle, ponytail and all, made him look lean and dangerous, and she wondered what it would be like to make love to Gage in his disguise. Her heart leaped and something hot pulsed low and deep inside her.

The man was a freaking iceberg. And ridiculously, Roxanne found herself admiring him.

"I've begun the process. We'll continue for three months. A quick hit is best for our resources as well as a way to avoid legal problems."

Just shows what you know, you creep. The law's already on your tail, and we're not letting—

We? Get a grip, girl.

"Mettles has the technical details worked out to perfection. My team and I will handle distribution. I have my own capital invested, naturally, but I prefer diversification, so your cash would be welcome."

Gage merely smiled—though not in the charming way she was used to. "How much?"

The two men spent the next twenty minutes discussing money, procedures and information exchange. Roxanne's head swam, then pounded, then went into a full holding pattern, especially when Clark launched into a discussion of the latest designer-shoe trends. If Mr. MIT-computer engineer thought he was going to distract her with swanky labels and the latest in jeweled sandals, he hadn't glanced at her strictly local-mall-inspired-and-budgeted wardrobe lately.

But as she listened to Gage and Stephano with one side of her brain, with the other side she recalled her role in this farce and fought to remember the latest excerpt from *InStyle* magazine.

This undercover business was *exhausting*.

And that was her last coherent thought as Gage's hand slid from the top of her thigh to her crotch. Beneath the tablecloth, no one else could have had any idea of the position of his hand or his...talents in subversive arousal.

Her stomach quivered. Her crotch went damp. She shifted uneasily on her seat and cut her gaze to Gage's, silently warning him to take a big step back.

Which, of course, he ignored.

Instead, he used his index finger to stroke her through the stretchy fabric of her suit.

She jumped on the seat, then surreptitiously jabbed Gage in the side, while still trying to maintain the trail of her and Mettles's conversation. "So, uh...uh..."

"Clark," Gage provided.

"Clark," she said, glaring at Gage out of the corner of her eye. "Who's your favorite designer?"

Clark pursed his lips. "Well, you can't beat the Italians..."

Gage flicked his finger over Roxanne's clitoris.

"Ah..."

"Oh, yes," Clark continued, oblivious to the true meaning behind her sigh. "I agree. Ferragamo is a certified genius."

Gage deepened his caress, gliding his finger back and forth, slowly, then faster. Roxanne's breath caught in her throat. Sweat slid down her spine.

He was a dead man. If she ever go out of here—

A gentle pinch.

The coil of desire cinched tighter.

"As for the current furor over Blahnik and Choo..." Clark droned on.

The coil tightened. And tightened. Until Roxanne was so needy, so desperate, so dependent on Gage ending the torture, she was ready to scream with frustration and simultaneously beg for satisfaction.

Beg? Hold it just a second, sister. She wasn't begging that lying, deceitful Gage Dabon for *anything*.

And how dare he work her into a frenzy in the middle of an important case? When their lives were in danger. When she was at the end of her emotional and physical rope.

Then she realized Gage's slickness went way beyond her expectations. He knew exactly what he was doing, when and why. He wanted her vulnerable and beholden to him. To control her.

She clamped her legs together.

Gage actually flinched in surprise.

Knees quaking, she stood. "I'm going to the ladies' room." Whether surprised by her tone or her abrupt movement, the men rose as she scooted past Gage out of the booth.

In the rest room, with her eyes dilated and a golden-skinned stranger staring back at her, she reapplied her bright red lipstick, all the while breathing deeply, reminding herself she didn't need men. Or sex. And certainly not sex from one particular man.

Imagine, him thinking he could control her with her hormones. Ha! She rolled her shoulders back, then adjusted her padded bra.

Her legs buckled. She caught herself against the black-marble countertop.

Good grief, he was one hell of a man.

ON THE DRIVE BACK to the hotel, Gage thought of his father.

Maybe he just didn't want to dwell on his failure to distract Roxanne. He'd wanted to remind her how he could make her feel, how great things had been between them, how she couldn't just throw all that away.

So, instead, sunk into the plush leather seats of Stephano's limo, he considered dear ol' dad.

His boss. Their odd connection and relationship. The relationship as compared to Roxanne and her father. He and his father were so much the same. Yet complete opposites.

Each trying to impress, fighting for attention and justice. His challenge for his own father's respect was more forward and apparent. They were in the same business. Boss and subordinate. Father and son.

Roxanne's situation was more subversive but no less obvious. She wanted her dad to understand what she did and why she did it, as much as she tried *not* to understand what he did and why he did it. She was a concerned citizen. Paid her taxes, valiantly pulled her car over to the right for the police and their sirens and lights, sympathized with their fight for justice, for the rights of victims. Even as she despised every case her father fought for.

As she mourned her mother.

As she hated her father for the life that brought her both love and pain.

This conflict of feelings fascinated him, drew him to her from the first. As punishment for his own choices, or as solace?

His mother had left, too, though not in the same tragic, uncontrollable way as Roxanne's. His mother had left of her own accord. Refusing to accept any longer a husband with single-minded dedication to justice. Or the son she'd birthed. She'd tried for ten years, but couldn't deal with the life of waiting by the phone, for the call of death or disappearance to come, and the boy could hardly blame her. His father could be cold and ruthless. Not the kind of man for a tender, suburban-loving wife. But as he'd always had his father's eyes, his father's attention to detail and quiet observance, his mother hadn't been willing to try with him either.

So, she'd left.

And he—as a boy and a man—had been alone.

His father wasn't much company. Oh, he'd seen to his son's schoolwork, made sure Gage steered clear of drugs and alcohol, drove him to football and baseball practice, allowed him friends and entertainment. But Gage had never really known the man, never really sensed an emotional or even intellectual connection.

Until the moment, at age fifteen, he'd caught his father in the bathroom, donning bright blue contacts.

The truth of his work had come out. The depth of his father's trust at such a young age still astounded him. These days, Gage would never be so trusting. But, in giving his young son his secret of undercover police work, Colin MacDonald had also created a legacy. Unmatched to this day and with a success rate other agents and agent teams only dreamed about.

Only in recent months, since Roxanne had entered his life, had Gage begun to question that legacy. His father had his only son's last name legally changed to hide their connection to the outside world. He'd taught him to lie, to become someone he wasn't. Just who had his father served? And why?

He and Roxanne had so much in common. And, yet, nothing at all. His reconciliation of that, or not, he sensed, would cost him his life.

5

ROXANNE SLAMMED the hotel-room door. "I've just about had it up to here—"

Gage clamped his hand over her mouth.

"Mmmf!" That arrogant, overbearing man had really gone too far this time.

"Bugs," he whispered in her ear.

There better be one helluva cockroach in the bathroom—

"Stephano can hear us."

Talk about a giant cockroach.

She simply nodded, and Gage moved his hand.

She stood, arms crossed, watching as Gage pulled a small device from his briefcase. He roamed the room, ostensibly searching for bugs.

Still angry with him for touching her in the restaurant, and even angrier at herself for her response, she fumed in silence. She'd really wanted to call him on the carpet the moment they were alone, and now her simmering fury had to bubble even longer. The delay didn't bode well for her undercover lover.

He found three in all—two in the living area and one in the bedroom. He balanced the tiny, round objects in his palm and held his hand out to her. "It's safe to talk now."

She glanced at the bugs and suppressed a shiver.

Frankly, she'd rather have the cockroach. "Won't they be suspicious their bugs aren't working?"

Gage closed his palm. "They'll know I'm not stupid."

As he crossed to his briefcase and stored the bugs and device thingy he'd detected them with, Roxanne drew a deep breath. She held on to her anger like a shield. "Just what the hell did you think you were doing at the restaurant?"

He flopped onto the sofa. "Making a deal with Stephano."

She stormed across the room, stopping next to him, glaring down at his relaxed position. "That's not what I meant and you know it."

He shrugged. "I figured you were nervous, so I tried to distract you, relax you."

"There was absolutely nothing remotely relaxing about—"

"There would have been if you'd given me two more minutes," he pointed out, then had the nerve to smile.

She didn't, couldn't say anything for several long moments. "You really are an arrogant son of a bitch, aren't you?"

He closed his eyes. "You ought to get some sleep. Tomorrow's going to be a long day."

"Oh, no, you don't." She grabbed his hand, jerking him to a sitting position. "We're having this out right—"

In a heartbeat, she was on her back, her arms pinned over her head and Gage straddling her. His eyes blazed into hers. His breath rushed out in hot gasps. As if she'd wakened a sleeping panther.

"You really don't want to push me just now, Roxanne."

Her heart thudded, but, strangely, she wasn't scared. She was aroused. Again.

"I've spent the last several hours watching those two revolting idiots drool over you, put their hands on you and continually suggest activities with you that I'd like to kill them for simply thinking much less voicing."

Gage is jealous. As dire as their situation was, and as angry as she was, and as over as their relationship was, she couldn't help the feminine thrill that raced through her body.

"And all the while," he continued, "you're playing your part by fawning over me, teasing me, touching me." He drew a deep breath. "All I have to do is smell you to get hard, and you've been two inches from me for hours. So, I'm just about at my breaking point. You'd be wise to just leave me the hell alone."

Pulse racing, she looked up at him, at the fierce, almost tortured expression on his face. And the gentle part inside her—the part of her heart she feared Gage would always own—sighed.

She wriggled her hand free, then slowly, tentatively, she drew her palm down his cheek. "I'm so sorry. I—"

"Don't," he said through clenched teeth, recapturing her hand.

Touch him, she assumed. She'd like to have pointed out that there was very little of their bodies that *weren't* touching at the moment, but somehow she sensed Gage wasn't in the mood for logic.

Especially since having his hard arousal pressed

against her stomach was so pleasurable. She sensed she trembled on the edge of tapping into that dark, troubled, dangerous side of Gage Dabon, the side she craved yet dreaded.

Pushing aside her cautious nature, she arched her back slightly, pressing her hips against his crotch.

His hands, wrapped around her wrists, clenched. His gaze bored into hers. "Don't push me," he said very quietly.

Her eyes challenging, she licked her lips.

Though she'd half expected the move, she gasped when his lips crushed down on hers. His spicy scent filled her head, his taste filled her mouth. The sophisticated tenderness she'd always associated with Gage was gone. In his place was a hungry, angry male, determined to reassert his control and domination over her.

And the very idea that she had him—all of him— aroused her beyond anything she believed possible. She'd always considered lovemaking a pleasurable extension of her feelings for Gage. He was a wonderful, considerate, gentle lover. She was a controlled person, a Southern lady who didn't run wild and loose. But whatever part of him she'd uncovered tonight seemed to exist in her as well.

Fever for him invaded her blood. She wrenched her hands free of his hard grip and grasped the front of his shirt, kneading it against her palms. The tangle of their tongues seemed to echo the battle of wills they'd started.

He cupped her breast, and she cried out.

He ripped apart the front of her cat suit, and she sighed.

Every erogenous zone in her body quivered. Her breasts ached for the scrape of his fingers, the moisture of his tongue. Her stomach needed the warmth of his skin, the sweat rolling off his abs and onto hers. Wet heat had flooded her sex, and she wanted him to fill her more than she wanted to draw her next breath. Desire had coiled so deeply inside her, she feared she'd never find relief.

He slid his mouth down her neck, his teeth and his tongue shooting sparks of desire higher. When he bit her ear, she arched her neck, silently begging for more. After flicking open the front clasp of her bra, he continued his blissful assault down her chest, taking first one, then the other nipple in his mouth, laving the tips with dampness, sinking his teeth lightly into them.

She buried her hands in his hair, clutching the silken strands so tightly she had no doubt she was hurting him. But he said nothing. Seemed not to notice. His focus was all for her. On her. Within her.

The tip of his tongue slid from her nipple, over the downward slope of her breast, the across her rib cage. When he reached the center of her stomach, dipping his tongue into her belly button, her breath caught. *Oh, my.* Their sensual explorations had rarely ventured in this direction, and always when Gage was at his most gentle. How would it feel now when—

He thrust his tongue directly between her slick folds.

"Oh, my—"

Ripples of sensations, the beginnings of her climax, started to roll outward. Then, just as suddenly as the caress began, he withdrew his tongue.

Her muscles clamped, reaching for the satisfaction they craved.

Oh, no, he wouldn't. He couldn't be cruel. She shook her head as the stillness lengthened, with her hovering at a precipice she had no hope of falling off.

But just as quickly as his touch was gone, his wonderful mouth was back. And the sensations magnified tenfold.

She clutched the sofa cushions, her fingers digging into the fabric. Her muscles tightened. She held her breath, praying for the delicious torture to end.

Then the tension broke, and she soared.

Her orgasm tore through her body without gentleness or subtlety. It pounded, demanded, and drained the very life out of her. She was pretty sure she even blacked out for a second or two.

When she opened her eyes, she was alone. Groggy, she sat up. "Gage?"

He walked in from the bedroom with a white robe tossed over his arm. Holding it toward her, he said, "Let's tuck you in bed."

She blinked. The last few minutes had been incredible, but she wanted the whole shebang. Didn't he? "But... You..."

He glanced away. "I shouldn't have touched you."

"You *regret* touching me?"

His gaze met hers straight on. "I had to finish what I started earlier."

"But you don't want to make love?"

"You need your rest."

The man was a damn professional at avoiding questions. Hurt and confused, she gathered the tatters of her cat suit around her, then stood, angrily thrusting her arms into the sleeves of the robe. "You sure seemed enthused a few minutes ago."

He ran his hands down her arms. "I was rough. I shouldn't have—"

She whirled. "Don't say that again."

Regret slid through his eyes. "I hurt you."

"No."

"Yes, I have."

His deception. The future they'd never have. He *had* hurt her. "Not physically," she countered.

In answer, he grabbed her hand and led her into the bathroom. He stood behind her as she faced the mirror.

Red marks marred the pale skin of her throat and chest. She cinched the belt on her robe and turned away from her reflection and the self-directed censure in Gage's eyes. "You didn't hurt me," she insisted.

"I *attacked* you. I *ripped* your clothes."

She stepped closer to him and cupped his cheek in her palm. "I *liked* it."

His eyes darkened.

"I always knew you had a dark side," she went on in a whisper. "And tonight I got to touch it."

"No." He stepped back, shuttering his thoughts and feelings with obvious longtime expertise. "I simply got too carried away. It's the stress of the case. I'll keep myself under better control from now on." He started to turn away.

She grabbed his arm. "No, dammit. You're not shutting me out. I don't want Mr. Cool and Controlled. I want the unleashed hunger I had out there." She jabbed her finger in the direction of the living room.

"I'm tired of you protecting me and coddling me. I'm tired of lies. I want all of you."

"I thought you didn't want me at all."

"I—" She closed her mouth. She didn't want him. She was helping him through this weekend. That's it. Then bye-bye, Gage Angelini, or whoever the hell he was and would be. She hadn't planned to complicate things with sex.

So why in the world was he reminding her she'd rejected a physical relationship between them? He certainly hadn't liked her calling off the engagement. Then, his eyes had been determined, as if she wouldn't find dumping him quite so easy. In fact, she was pretty darn sure his arousal under the table had been his way of reminding her that she *did* want him. That their sex life was an area they managed extremely well.

Had he suddenly decided she wasn't worth the trouble to keep? She'd always had insecurities in that area, and twenty-four hours ago she would have bought that excuse lock, stock and barrel.

But tonight she had the feeling she'd just hit too close to the mark with her touching his bad-side comment.

Good grief. Had she actually said that? Like quoting a bad line from a *Star Wars* movie. *Feel the Force, Gage.*

Exhaustion had finally claimed her brain.

She wasn't likely to puzzle her way through Gage's motives tonight. And, hey, she'd definitely gotten the good end of the deal in the orgasm department. She'd told him the whole experience was pretty cool for her. If he wanted to martyr himself and brood, fine by her.

Shrugging, she ushered Gage out of the bathroom.

"I'm taking a bath, then going to bed. Make sure I don't miss breakfast."

As she closed the door, his puzzled frown was the last thing she saw.

LONG AFTER ROXANNE was in bed, Gage lay on the sofa, shoved a thin pillow behind his head and let loose a stream of expletives. He started in English, then moved on to Italian, French, Spanish, and wound things up with a touch of German.

"Women are a pain in the ass," he muttered into the silent, darkened room.

He'd tried to be noble, to apologize for turning into a crazed animal, for shamelessly manipulating her body into wanting him, for trying to brand her as his, and only his, woman forever.

And what did he get in return? Psychoanalysis.

He snorted. His dark side? *Please*.

He'd just been using sex to keep her under his control, to remind her she wanted him despite all the reasons her complicated female brain had given her not to.

You just don't like how close she was. And I don't mean physically.

"Oh, shut up," he told his conscience.

He was a man. Using sex to get his way was as natural as breathing.

You pushed her away because she's not supposed to be part of the darkness. She's the only light in your miserable life.

He wanted to scoff, to turn off the part of him that always found a way to the brutal, honest truth.

But he couldn't. He *didn't* want her part of the very

real dark side of his life. The lies. The scum. The danger.

But he also reveled in the idea that the dark passion inside him had escaped, and Roxanne hadn't turned away from him. She hadn't been shocked or scared.

I liked it.

Recalling her words, he went instantly hard, and so he sighed in disgust. So much for the cold shower he'd tortured himself with.

It had taken a long, frigid dip in the water to chill his earlier desire. After bringing Roxanne to climax, he'd wanted to drive himself into her more than he wanted to draw his next breath, but then he'd seen the marks on her neck. And he'd been disgusted. He'd lost it, and he feared hurting her further, overwhelming her, and, yes, letting her get too close.

Better to rein in that wild, uncontrollable side and remind himself he had to stay focused on this case and their safety, not his dick.

No way in hell was he getting back in that shower. So, he turned his thoughts to the case. A vision of Stephano leering at Roxanne steered his energy into anger rather than sex.

He'd learned a valuable piece of information during dinner that evening. From the way Stephano kept referring to his base of operations—the supply warehouse where the bills were manufactured—Gage knew it had to be close, probably in downtown New Orleans. Like hiding in plain sight. People came and went in the Quarter at all hours of the day and night. No one would question delivery trucks or workers at 2:00 a.m., seedy-looking henchmen or a pocket protector–carrying engineer.

Gage's father had a lot of contacts at NOPD and knew several local judges. If he could get a lock on this warehouse—admittedly a monumental challenge—he could have a search warrant within an hour. Then all he had to do was catch Stephano inside—like *that* would be easy—and this whole mess would be over.

And Roxanne could officially walk out of his life forever.

Great. Then my life will be perfect.

A perfect, miserable disaster.

"GAGE, I want to break up."

Gage paused with his scrambled egg–laden fork halfway to his mouth. "Come again?"

Across from him, looking as serene as a priest at Sunday mass and still wearing a hotel bathrobe, Roxanne laid her engagement ring in the center of the table. "Officially."

Numb, he laid down his fork. He couldn't seem to tear his gaze from the sparkling, pear-shaped diamond surrounded by small emeralds. "Why?" he managed to ask.

She drew a deep breath. "After last night, I realized I've given you some mixed signals. I'm pretending to be involved with you while Stephano is around, but when we're alone, I don't want any…physical contact between us. I know it will be difficult, but I think it's best, given the circumstances."

Everything inside Gage had gone cold. "Circumstances?"

"I'm staying here and helping you, but once you have Stephano in custody…I'd like you to move out of the house."

He finally looked up, finding her golden-brown gaze locked on his face. Marina was gone and sweet Roxanne was back, so how could she sit there so calmly, so unemotionally, and destroy him?

"I'm sorry, Gage. I just can't live my life with a cop. I promised myself a long time ago."

He fought the urge to beg. "What if I wasn't a cop?"

"But you are."

"What if I quit?"

Her eyes widened briefly, then she shook her head. "You can't stop being something you are. I won't ask you to."

"It's just a job."

"No, it's not."

True, he'd considered himself a cop for so long, he couldn't imagine changing his view. His job was a part of him in a way that he suspected most people would never understand. It encompassed his whole identity.

But he was pretty sure losing Roxanne would kill him.

She laid her hand over his, then, as he glanced down, she moved it. Obviously, even hand-holding was too much physical contact. "I'm sorry, Gage. Are you upset or relieved?"

He stood, turning away from her and thrusting his hand through his hair. "I'm not relieved." He looked back at her. "*Why* would I be relieved?"

"I'm not exactly ideal for a man like you."

"A man like me."

Her face flushed. "You know, sophisticated, confident, gorgeous. You could have any woman you want."

"I want you." Admittedly not a flowery, and certainly not a sophisticated, declaration, but it was all he could manage at the moment.

Though pleasure lit her eyes briefly, his confession didn't seem to sway her in the least. "Why? We're complete opposites. After yesterday, that's even more obvious."

"Opposites attract," he said, wanting to wince at the pat answer.

She shook her head. "Why else?"

Why couldn't he put his feelings into words? He hadn't done it in so long, he'd probably forgotten how. His father wasn't much for easy affection. And though he'd written countless letters to his mother for three years after she'd left, telling her how much he needed her and wanted her back, she'd never come back.

She rose from the table. "The pause is long enough."

He crossed to her. "Dammit, I don't know why I do, I just do." He reached for her, but she stepped back. "We're good together."

"I don't belong with you, Gage."

A knock on the door forestalled whatever idiotic response Gage could come up with next.

"Get in the bedroom," he said as he scooped his Beretta off the entryway table. When she ignored his command, he cursed, then peered out the peephole in the door.

Nobody.

Damn. Had he tipped too much to Stephano? He'd let Roxanne distract him, worrying too much about his love life instead of his *life* life. He flattened his back against the wall beside the door, flipping off the pistol's safety and sliding his finger against the trigger. "Who is it?"

"Room service," said a fake-sounding deep voice.

His heart thudded. "They've already been here."

"Hell, Gage, it's me, Toni. Open the door."

Recognizing her real voice, Gage cursed again and opened the door, grabbing Toni's hand and pulling her around the door as he flicked the safety back on his pistol and tucked it behind his back before she noticed it.

Like Roxanne, she was back to normal this morning. The skintight outfit and hooker-blond wig were gone, replaced by a lime-green silk tank dress and her own shaggy, medium-blond hair. And her diamond-hard blue gaze was aimed directly at him. "I'm here to get Roxanne."

Hadn't he decided last night women were a pain in the ass?

He flopped onto the sofa, hiding his gun between the cushions. "Fine by me."

Roxanne glared at him as she crossed to her friend. "Have some coffee."

"Already had two cups, thanks."

"Which explains why you're so irritable. How about some breakfast? We have plenty."

Gage laid his head back against the cushion and closed his eyes, trying to block out their chatter. He didn't have the patience for this.

"How's the rehearsal going?" Toni asked.

"What rehearsal?" Roxanne returned.

"The Ponytail That Roared," Gage said without opening his eyes.

"Oh, that. Well, we're taking a break."

"Uh-huh," Toni said, sounding as if she didn't believe a word.

And, really, who would? Roxanne was a lousy liar. Though she'd held her ground well last night with Stephano and Mettles. Held her ground? Hell, she'd flourished. He had little doubt Stephano's lust for "Marina", along with his natural pride, had caused him to reveal more than was wise. They could make a powerful team.

But he wanted her as far away from Stephano and his like as he could get her.

And all she wanted was to be as far away from *him* as she could get.

He had to do something to change her mind. He couldn't lose her. He needed her light and sweetness and vulnerability. He needed her laughter and stability. Her intelligence. Her *body*.

He *could* quit. Retire. He'd been thinking about leaving more every day, more about normality and building something permanent and strong. He couldn't imagine his life without a case to solve, but he'd been at this crap long enough to wonder if he really made a difference anyway.

What would he do, though? Open a hardware store? Build birdhouses? Could he really leave behind the only purpose he'd ever felt in his life? And if he did, and Roxanne took him back, would he someday resent her?

You can't stop being something you are.

Could he?

"Gage, are you asleep?" Roxanne asked suddenly.

"No." He kept his eyes closed.

"Have you been listening?"

"Yes. Toni wants to take you with her. She thinks I'm bad for you. You assured her we're having a romantic weekend, which would be going more smoothly if Toni would go home. Oh, and she thinks the play is bullshit."

"Should we explain further?"

"No."

Someone sat beside him. Close. Roxanne. She smelled delicious, and the warmth of her body seeped into his. Someone should tell her to move back a few paces. Maybe a few blocks. His nerves were already strung out to the point of snapping, and he was perilously close to flinging her over his shoulder and kidnapping her until she saw reason with their relationship. He blanked out the picture of her engagement ring lying in the center of the table.

"I think we should tell her," Roxanne whispered in his ear. "She's not going away."

Gage finally opened his eyes and glanced at her. God, it was painful to look at her, knowing he'd lost her. "Tell her what?"

She rolled her eyes. "You know."

"No."

"I really don't think we can get rid of her."

"I could have four Federal Agents at the door of her shop in twenty minutes on suspicion of trafficking."

"Trafficking what?"

"Anything."

"Have I told you lately that this ruthless side of yours bothers me?"

"Last night it turned you on."

She glared at him. "Last night it didn't exist at all according to you, and you're changing the subject. If we just tell her, she'll go away. What if she pops up again while we're with the bad guys?"

He realized suddenly how much he liked the change in her over the last twelve hours. She never would have argued this strenuously before. And he never could have imagined having a conversation with her about a case. Embarrassingly, he realized he wouldn't have expected her to understand or be interested in his cases.

And while she'd told him she wanted him out of her life, she sure wasn't running out—even with her best friend tugging her. She was staying with him, seeing this mess through. If she cared so little for him, why was she helping him?

Last night Stephano would have been royally pissed if she hadn't shown up, and he might even have taken out his frustration on Gage. But today she could go. She didn't have to see this through.

He should send her with Toni. She'd be safe. But she'd be gone. And he suspected if he let her walk out that door right now, he'd never get her back.

Selfish? Of course. But he'd never claimed to be a saint.

"No one besides my father and a few higher-ups in the government know who I really am, Rox. No way am I telling two women in two days."

"I think that's an insult to my gender."

"I trust you, I just—"

"Romantic weekend, huh?" Toni commented suddenly. "Then what is this doing here?" With a pleased smirk on her face, she held up Roxanne's engagement ring.

6

WELL, DAMN.

Roxanne's mind scrambled for a legitimate excuse, even as she tried to figure out how to cover things up without putting that ring back on. She'd made a decision, and she was very afraid of weakening—she was still feeling *extremely* weak where Gage was concerned—and she didn't want to pretend with the symbol of their relationship. Last night she'd even tucked the sapphire necklace he'd given her in her purse.

Thankfully, her smooth, quick-thinking lover—*that's ex-lover, remember*—came to her rescue.

Slick as butter sliding across a hot roll, he strolled over to Toni and took the ring, tucking the diamond into his front pocket. "Roxanne's lost a bit of weight over the last few weeks, so her ring is loose. Of course, I offered to have it resized." His eyebrows rose. "Really, Toni, making something out of a bit of nothing, aren't we?"

Then he crossed back to Roxanne and tipped her face up for his kiss. His silver eyes glinted with mischief, obviously enjoying the performance. As his mouth settled over hers, she couldn't deny how much she craved his touch. What had she done, breaking up with him? She'd been prepared to marry him, for better or for worse. Hell, forever. She was Catholic after all.

When he pulled away, he ran his thumb across her bottom lip. There was no denying the desire in his eyes. "I'm grabbing a shower, darling. Then let's go shopping."

Good grief, that man packs a powerful punch.

She angled her head sideways, watching him walk from the room. In a black T-shirt and blue jeans. She searched her memory, but came up blank in the Gage-wearing-jeans department. Even around the house on weekends, he was always dressed like a character from an F. Scott Fitzgerald novel. Of course, that was Gage Dabon, financial adviser, consummate sophisticate. She was dealing with Gage Angelini now. Rough, ruthless rebel.

She shivered in delight.

"You wanna tell me what the hell is going on now?"

Roxanne turned to Toni, who had her hands propped on her curvy hips and that too-familiar determined expression on her face. "Don't start."

"What are you shopping for?"

Already tired of arguing, Roxanne sank into her chair at the breakfast table. "Clothes. I didn't bring any with me last night, remember?"

Toni braced her hand on the table and leaned close to Roxanne. "Just go home and get some. You only live five miles away."

"Toni, a man with at least three platinum Visa cards that I know of wants to take me shopping. Why would I argue with him?"

"Ah-ha!" She waggled her finger. "I *knew* you were up to something. You wouldn't know a Valentino from an Armani. You don't even *like* shopping."

"I can't share this with you," Roxanne said quietly,

meeting her best friend's gaze. And saw surprise and hurt. "I'm sorry. All I can tell you is that I have to stay here with Gage for the weekend. And even on Monday, I can't really explain everything."

"We've been best friends since we were five, Rox."

"I know." Tears clogged her throat. It would be so nice to share with someone, but knowing Gage's secret life had left her very much alone. Though she knew she could trust her life—and his—with Toni, she wouldn't betray his confidence. Toni's anger would burn hot, and not for long, but maybe long enough to send her home until after the weekend. She couldn't get her friend mixed up in all this, too.

Toni straightened, then turned away. "If that's the way you feel."

"That's the way it has to be," Roxanne said miserably to her friend's back.

Toni walked out, closing the door quietly behind her.

Minutes later, when Gage walked into the room, Roxanne still hadn't moved. A hollow ache had invaded her heart.

"Where's Toni?"

She sniffled. "Gone."

"Rox, are you all—" Gage was kneeling in front of her before the next syllable was out of his mouth.

She threw her arms around his neck and held on as the tears started with a vengeance.

He stroked her back and kissed the top of her head. "It's okay, baby. It's the stress. You're going to be fine. I'm here."

"I'm n-not s-supposed to be t-touching you."

"We can make an exception this once."

She cried harder. Maybe she was losing her mind. Having a nervous breakdown. Other people had them. Toni's mother had them on a weekly basis.

"Oh, T-Toni. She's s-so mad at m-me."

Gage held her tighter. "She'll get over it."

Maybe. When this was all over, she could get back in Toni's good graces, but Gage would be out of her life. Last night she was so sure she'd made the right decision, but this morning, watching his silver eyes darken with what she could have sworn was pain, she'd begun to doubt herself. If she could hurt him, he must care.

But he hadn't given her the assurances she needed. She'd wanted him to declare his undying love, that he'd do anything to keep her.

And then what, Rox? He'd still be a cop. Even if he was a florist he'd be a cop. She couldn't ask him to change, didn't want him to. She just couldn't live her life with him.

Logical thinking helped her get control of her emotions. She wiped her tears with the collar of her robe. "My face probably looks like a tomato."

He smiled. "You look beautiful. As always."

"I think I'm through falling apart now."

"Glad to hear it. I need you in one piece."

Her eyes widened. "Do you really need me?"

"Definitely. You were great last night. At the restaurant," he added, obviously distinguishing from all that had occurred at the hotel.

"I was really helpful?"

"You were just the distraction I needed for Stephano." He rose, then retrieved his gun from between the sofa cushions, where he must have hidden it when

Toni arrived. "I think he let his guard down a bit, and I uncovered some promising information."

She followed him across the room, noting he'd changed out of the jeans and T-shirt and into an expensive-looking black silk shirt and black slacks. He was going shopping in New Orleans in *that?*

Not only would he roast, she'd been looking forward to ogling his backside in those jeans all day.

"What information?" she asked to distract herself. Ogling definitely fell into the off-limits category, right after "no physical contact."

"Just an aspect of the case I needed to clarify," he said absently as he set his pistol in his briefcase before retrieving a small revolver, which he slid into an ankle holster.

"What aspect?"

"I need to check in with headquarters, then we'll get going."

She planted herself in his path. "What aspect?"

"I can't really—"

"If I'm in this, I know what you know."

Instead of arguing, as she expected him to, he simply sighed. "I think his center of operations is here in New Orleans."

That was a big revelation? She resisted the urge to say, "Well, duh!"

He must have read the bafflement on her face. "Mettles just got here two days ago. Stephano arrived yesterday. Before that, I tracked him to Aruba, before that—"

"Wait just a damn second. You left here *five* days ago. You were in *Aruba* instead of Chicago?"

In the process of pulling a laptop from his briefcase,

he paused. "I refuse to answer that question on the grounds it might incriminate me."

"Uh-huh. And here I thought your skin was just naturally swarthy. Ha!"

"I had electronic surveillance set up in my hotel room. I didn't spend my days lying on the beach except—"

Her blood pressure shot up another few notches. "Except?"

"Except for the few hours I posed as a hotel pool waiter."

"Oh, a hotel pool waiter." She crossed her arms over her chest, reveling in the I've-got-him-on-the-ropes power. Her nipples even hardened. She wanted to be embarrassed by her reaction, but found the opposite occurred. She felt bold and confident. "Well...a hotel pool waiter has a *strenuous* job. Carrying drinks. Chatting with resort guests. Checking out babes in bikinis."

He grinned. "You're jealous."

She stepped closer to him. Only a few inches separated their bodies. She could smell the sharpness of his aftershave. "I am not."

"You are." He tucked the laptop under his arm. "It's cute."

"It's—" She was talking to his back as he crossed to the breakfast table and pushed aside the dishes to make room for his computer. She went after him, facing him and her anger. "I am not *cute*." The fact that he looked sexy and sophisticated, and she was wearing a bathrobe and no makeup also irked the hell out of her. "I just want to be an equal in this. If I'm risking my ass for you, I want your respect. I don't want to be treated like a fainting female." She ignored the fact that she'd just spent twenty minutes crying in his arms. "I want to know what's going on."

"You're sexy as hell when you're pissed off, Rox."

"Really? You're not so bad yourself."

"So, HONEY, do you think we can find Joe's little store?"

After much discussion, and Gage revealing more about the case than was probably wise, they'd decided on Roxanne and Toni's original plan—tourists on the make. While searching for a counterfeiting warehouse. "We'll see, baby."

Roxanne crossed her legs within the close confines of the cab, and Gage glanced out the window. If he saw another inch of her legs, he wouldn't be able to get out of the car with any measure of decency. He'd always thought Roxanne's legs were a never-ending, lust-inducing aspect of her body, but with her wig and contacts, he found himself delving deep into the fantasy of the sophisticated bad girl. So, his mind wandered. His libido jumped to attention, and a ball of lust had settled deep inside, ready to spring at the least provocation.

No physical contact? Ha! He didn't see how it was possible to stick to that little dictum.

Of course, if he got her to touch him first...

As the cab inched toward the French Quarter, Roxanne leaned toward him. "Where did you get this outfit? Victoria's Secret?"

Since she'd been wearing a bathrobe before he'd ventured around the corner from the hotel to get makeup, bronzing powder, tanning cream and find her something to wear, he didn't understand why she was complaining. But then he glanced again at the short, skintight miniskirt and wraparound red shirt covering—though barely—her curves. Well, maybe he'd gotten a little carried away...

"The shop had T-shirts, personalized pencils and shot glasses, Mardi Gras masks and hot sauce. Believe me, that was the best thing around."

"Did you have to get something so short and tight?"

Well, no. But she looked *really* great in his selection. "You're playing a part, remember?"

"I think you're enjoying this part a little too much."

He managed to look offended. "Darling, I'm a professional."

"A professional scoundrel," she muttered, then turned her head to look out the window.

Knowing she wanted to—and thought she could—dismiss him, Gage whispered in her ear, careful not to touch, but making sure his breath stirred the tendrils of hair curled along her neck. "A scoundrel who wants to get between your lovely long legs more than he wants to draw his next breath."

As expected, she sucked in a breath and whipped her head around to face him, bringing their faces within inches of each other. "We agreed..."

He smiled. "No, you suggested. I agreed to nothing."

Her green gaze searched his face, her expression wary, but he also thought he detected a hint of longing. "Please, Gage."

He deliberately dropped his gaze to her lips. "Please what?"

"Be reasonable."

"No."

Her gaze flicked to his lips.

She's weakening.

"Chartres and St. Peters," the cabdriver announced.

Far from disappointed with the opening to his seduction, Gage slid money over the seat to the driver, then scooted out of the cab. He held out his hand to Roxanne and waited until she laid her hand in his before he assisted her out of the car. Once she stood on the sidewalk, he released her. He'd pretend to play by the rules—for a while anyway.

Passing the St. Louis Cathedral, they started down the crowded street, skirting a crowd of college kids all sporting half-full plastic cups of alcoholic Hurricanes. At eleven o'clock in the morning. Gage shook his head at the enthusiasm of youth.

"I'm going to break my ankles walking in these shoes," Roxanne said.

Gage glanced down at the black high-heeled pumps she was currently trying to balance between cracks in the sidewalk. "Shoes first, then."

As they continued down the street, he was careful to slow his stride so she could keep up easier, even as he scanned the area for buildings and shops large enough to hold Stephano's operation. Since nearly everything was done via computer these days, printing counterfeit bills from plates required specialized equipment. No one used the metal plates of old, but other agents inside the investigation had received information that Stephano had gotten his hands on a pair of old hundred-dollar and twenty-dollar plates that had been stolen several years ago, then had them modified to bring them up to current standards. The original theft was what had touched off the investigation in the beginning, and Stephano hadn't even been a suspect then. Gage had only been brought in six months ago when the lead about Stephano had come in. For the past few months, they'd run in circles, chasing Stephano and learning little to nothing about whether he had originally stolen the plates and why, since no counterfeit money had yet been circulated.

But all the theories connected to the plates seemed moot the moment Gage had discovered Mettles's involvement. Running the printing machines wouldn't require an MIT-educated computer engineer.

Though he hadn't shared his theory with anyone at the department yet, Gage didn't think the stolen plates had anything to do with Stephano's operation. Maybe he had swiped them, and even tried to use them in the operation. Maybe the plates were a decoy.

This case, though, was about technology. And if Mettles really did have the computer knowledge Gage suspected he did, this whole operation could be running with a modified laptop and printer sitting on a kitchen table. What he wanted to find today was the supply warehouse. Five properties in the area were owned by a subsidiary of one of Stephano's dummy corporations. Both he and the department figured Stephano had slid the counterfeiting supplies in with some of his other acquisitions—stolen computers, stereos and other electronics. Gage was to check out two of the locations, with two other agents looking into the other three.

With summer hovering on the horizon, and the city clogged with staggering numbers of tourists, who would notice a few more trucks and crates? And the timing was perfect to test the market and slide in a few fake bills. Since the mobster had commented last night about the operation lasting three months, it seemed summer was the target time.

But what was Stephano's overall plan? How was he going to make big money with his operation? He couldn't go around to every high-priced jewelry store in town and buy a million dollars in diamonds with fake money. Too obvious. Too risky. So, what—

"Don't you think we should, uh, hold hands or something?"

Still lost in his thoughts, he glanced at Roxanne. "Hold hands?"

She glared up at him out of her bright green eyes, flipping a strand of long black hair over her shoulder, and he was reminded again how well she'd slid into the role of the exotic Mediterranean beauty. "We're supposed to be, you know...together."

"Do you want to hold my hand, Marina?"

Though he could tell she'd rather slug him, she grabbed his hand and tugged him into a shoe store. "I want shoes."

Fifteen minutes later—and Gage had to admire the speed—she had a pair of sexy, strappy, low-heeled sandals, and he was out a hundred and fifteen bucks.

"So, where do you think we ought to start looking for Joe's?" she said matter-of-factly as they stood again on the crowded sidewalk.

I told her *my theory and not my boss.* If he didn't retire he'd probably get fired.

"I've got a few ideas."

She linked her arm through his, and they walked to the corner, where they waited for the light before

starting down the next block. Gage tried not to notice
how Roxanne's breast rubbed against his side with
each step they took. He tried to ignore the spicy scent
rising off her skin. He tried not to stare at the delicate
curve of her jaw, or how the makeup exaggerated her
eyes, so they seemed to dominate her fine-boned face.

He failed miserably on all points.

He *needed* to concentrate on the case. He *needed* to
find the warehouse and be alert in case Stephano
sicced a couple of his goons on their tail. He *needed* to
be ready if the agents watching Stephano or Mettles
reported anything significant.

He needed Roxanne.

"Close?" she asked next to his ear.

He swallowed and fought back a new wave of desire. "Half a block, but we're walking past then dou-
bling back." He just wanted to get an idea of what
flanked the property in case he needed to break in
later, and he couldn't have Stephano or his people
spotting Gage poking around.

"Oh, that's so exciting!" she said loudly, then whispered, "What number?"

"Forty-five."

Number forty-five was a small store with a dirty
front window and green and red paint peeling around
the frame. An old, pitiful-looking Christmas wreath
still hung on the door, and the sign hanging out front
read only "mas Depot." Obviously, the Christmas Depot had been gone for some time. On the left side of
the shop was a run-down T-shirt shop and on the right
a prominent-looking jewelry store.

Gage drew Roxanne to the jewelry-store window.

"How 'bout that necklace, baby?" He pointed at a diamond choker that probably made up ten karats.

Though her eyes popped wide, she giggled. "Oh, honey, I just *love* that one."

He slid his hand around hers and gave her an encouraging squeeze. "Let's try it on."

Inside the shop, a nicely dressed, soft-spoken elderly man introduced himself as Mr. Tanner, the owner. Roxanne picked up the ball without missing a beat, oohing and aahing over the sparkling gems in the long glass case dominating one wall, giving Gage the opportunity to wander, ostensibly to look at the art, crystal vases and porcelain figurines scattered around.

He noted the decent security system by the back door, which led into a small storeroom, then the alley. The only vehicle in the alley was a gray Volvo, conveniently parked with the plate visible. Gage made a mental note, then continued his tour around the room.

It was a nice shop with a quality, if smallish, inventory. He doubted Mr. Tanner had any idea a ruthless mobster was renting next door.

Approaching Roxanne from behind, he used the opportunity to slide his arm around her waist. "Find anything, baby?"

Several gaudy necklaces lay against black velvet. The diamond choker from the window. One with several large square rubies. One with sapphires. One with— He swallowed.

And one with a pear-shaped diamond surrounded by small emeralds hanging from a delicate gold chain.

It matched her engagement ring to a tee.

"The lady likes the choker," Mr. Tanner said, "but I

think this one matches her well." He pointed at the diamond and emerald necklace. "It goes perfectly with her eyes, don't you think, sir?"

His heart pounding, Gage glanced at Roxanne. Her eyes were stricken and focused on his face. "Yes, it does."

Mr. Tanner smiled, obviously sensing the close of the sale. "Would the lady like to try it on?"

Gage lifted Roxanne's hair off her neck as Mr. Tanner leaned forward to fasten the chain, but she stepped back suddenly, shaking her head. "I've...I've changed my mind. I don't want any jewelry." She stared over Gage's shoulder, careful not to meet his gaze. "Can we just go now?"

"Sure." Trying to hide his hurt over her rejection, and sensing she needed a moment to herself, he added, "I'll meet you outside."

The second she was out the door, he said to Mr. Tanner, "Wrap it up, please. I'll give it to her later."

Mr. Tanner nodded silently and proceeded to ring up the sale.

Outside, as the door closed behind him, Gage immediately started down the street, leaving Roxanne to follow.

She grabbed his arm, turning him to face her. "I'm sorry. Did I screw things up in there?"

"No." He started to move away again.

She held tight to his arm. "I'm sorry, Gage. You must know why I couldn't—"

"Forget it." He pulled his arm free and stalked down the sidewalk. He knew he was acting like an ass, but he was too pissed off at the moment to reason with himself. If she was so damn determined to throw his feelings, his ring and that damn necklace back in his face, maybe he should just let her. He'd been alone a long time. Maybe he wasn't cut out for happily-ever-after anyway. Just because he wanted marriage didn't mean he'd be good at it. He'd probably screw it up. He obsessed over his career and—

Hell, if there was a marriage, there wouldn't be a career.

Damn, he wanted a drink. And a damn aspirin.

Somehow, he had the presence of mind to find his way to the next address. He stormed past his target number eighty-eight—a florist—then stopped two doors down at ninety-two, a lingerie shop. Roxanne wouldn't like it, but the only other shop between the two addresses was an art gallery. He wasn't toting around a painting all afternoon.

"In here," he said as he held open the door.

She glanced at the sign—Ooh, Ah—and winced, but she strode inside.

Before he entered, Gage again glanced down to eighty-eight and noted a burly bald man pushing his way through the door. He'd seen that face before—on a mug shot. One of Stephano's henchmen.

Cursing and hoping he hadn't been seen, he slipped into the lingerie shop. The placed was filled with everything you'd need…if you were a hooker. Frilly lingerie, leather lingerie, hip boots, halter tops, hot pants, feather boas, and even variety-flavored condoms by the case. Of course, their primary customers might also be quiet, suburban couples, looking to add some spark to their love lives.

Gage certainly wouldn't object if Roxanne showed

up at the dinner table wearing one of those red lace hot pants and bra thingys hanging on the far wall.

Roxanne poked him in the back. "And just what do you think we're going to buy in here?" she asked in a low tone.

He turned and smiled sweetly. "Darling, it's just your style, don't you think?"

"Good morning." A small Oriental man bowed before them. "I will offer you assistance?" He smiled as he stared at Roxanne, showing a wide gap between his two front teeth.

Noting the bald guy exiting the florist's and heading their way, Gage strode quickly around the shop, randomly pulling items from the racks. "She'll try these on."

"Oh, no, I—"

"Bad guy at twelve o'clock," he whispered in Roxanne's ear. He hooked his arm around her waist and squeezed. "Dressing rooms?" he asked the clerk.

Still grinning, the man pointed to his left. "Back there."

Gage headed over, pulling a reluctant Roxanne along.

"No, sir." The little man hurried after them. "Only the lady can go back there."

Gage waved a handful of lingerie in his direction. "I'm her tailor. I need to supervise the fit." He urged Roxanne through a door, then behind a purple-curtained dressing room.

"Who's out there?" she whispered.

Shaking his head, Gage hung the clothes on a hook. "How about this one, baby?" He held up a hot-pink teddy, held together on the sides only by strings.

Roxanne crossed her arms over her chest and mouthed "no way."

Undaunted, Gage slid the outfit off its hanger. He didn't think the goon had seen him, but he wasn't taking any chances. They had to act like customers. Getting Roxanne undressed was just an added bonus. "Here you go," he said as he held the garment out to her.

She sighed in disgust and snatched the outfit. "Turn around."

"Hell, babe, I've seen—"

She made a circling motion with her finger.

The dressing room was small, so she had to brace her hand against his shoulder twice. He also hadn't anticipated the added thrill of hearing a zipper sliding down, clothes dropping to the floor, fabric rustling against skin and her quiet but labored breathing throughout the process.

He fought the arousal stealing its way through his body. He should be able to control his reaction to her. He'd always been in full control of his body and mind before he met her. But she left him weak and trembling, and that confused, irritated and pleased him all at the same time.

"All set," she finally announced.

He turned. His gaze caressed her, starting with her dark, curly hair falling past her shoulders and across one tanned breast. A breast barely covered by a scrap of pink satin, trimmed in lace, held up by a thin strap over her shoulder. The satin slid over her stomach, then, south of her belly button, the fabric became see-through, communicating quite vividly that black wasn't her natural hair color. His gaze pretty much froze right there.

"What do you think, sweetie?" she asked, smiling and cocking one hip.

"I, uh..." He shoved his hands in his pockets, clenching them into fists. He wanted to grab her. "It's great. Wrong color, though." He was already imagining it next to her pale skin and red hair. "How about the black one?"

Grumbling, she snatched that one off the hanger. He obligingly turned his back, and the process started all over again.

The black one was cotton, strapless and bared her stomach. Her hardened nipples poked against the fabric. *Oh, man.* The hip-hugger bottoms ended...

"Turn," he said, trying to look contemplative instead of hungry.

She turned her back, and sweat exploded all over his body when he noticed the bottoms ended before they'd fully covered her bottom.

"Don't you think this one's great, sweetie?" she asked, turning, her smile strained. She was either just as aroused as him or about to punch his lights out.

"The silver one," he choked out.

She huffed, and he faced the wall again, having no idea why he was torturing himself this way. Stephano's goon was probably long gone, and he obviously hadn't come into the store. All was quiet beyond the purple curtain. Roxanne probably thought he was a pervert.

The silver outfit was satin trimmed in sequins and boosted her breasts up so they were bared almost to her nipples. The bottoms were string bikini panties and also satin, riding just along her hipbones.

"Turn."

"No."

He met her gaze, noting her pupils were dilated, her cheeks flushed. She *was* aroused.

Okay, maybe this wasn't helping his case any, but it sure was helping his seduction plans. Roxanne had a terrific body, but she wasn't much for parading around the house in sexy underwear—not that she needed it to get his attention. Under normal circumstances she dressed elegantly and conservatively. But somehow these cheap, obvious clothes were getting to her. Maybe playing these roles excited her as much as him. Was the idea of being a bad girl a turn-on?

"Turn," he said again, this time making sure his gaze was locked with hers. *I dare you.*

She glared, but she turned.

And, oh, what a view it was.

The silver panties became a thin line of sequins in the back, disappearing between—

He leaned sideways, and she whacked him on the arm.

"I think this is it, don't you, dear?"

He straightened. "Oh, yeah."

Then they stood there, staring at each other. Him, fully dressed. Her, looking like something out of the Frederick's of Hollywood catalog. Him, needy and nearly desperate. Her... Well, he'd never know if he didn't try.

He yanked her into his arms, groaning when her scantily clad body slithered against his. "I need you," he confessed in a tight whisper.

She pressed her hips against him. "Gage, I—"

Before she could protest or think of a reason not to, he kissed her. He slid his tongue home. Against hers. Caressing hers.

He cupped the back of her neck with one hand, feeling the edge of her wig as he angled her head for deeper, better access. He tried to absorb her into him, desperate to show her how much her passion completed him. His other hand was wrapped tight around her waist, and the feel of her bare skin beneath his palm sent his own need soaring higher. His body pulsed.

With a groan, he backed her against the dressing-room wall. The old wood creaked, but Roxanne held on, her hands bracketing his waist.

Then he remembered the thong. He dropped his hands to her backside, cupping her cheeks in his palms, lifting her against the wall, pressing the juncture of her thighs against his hardness. The contact brought some relief while still managing to arouse him further.

She yanked his shirt from his pants and slid her hands beneath the fabric, rhythmically gliding her palms up and down his chest.

Desperate for air, he trailed his lips across her cheek, then down her jaw. "Rox," he whispered against her neck, absorbing her scent into his soul. Would he ever get this close to her again? He'd managed to overwhelm her today because of the proximity they were forced into. When tomorrow came, she'd leave him. Forever. "I need—"

"Sit," she gasped.

He immediately swung her around to the tiny

bench along the back wall, kneeling in front of her as he again captured her mouth.

But she pulled back. Her eyes were wild with arousal as they met his gaze. "*You* sit."

He sat beside her, holding tight to her waist, afraid to let go.

She dropped off the bench, kneeling on the floor between his knees.

Holy—

He stopped thinking as her gaze held his, and she lowered his zipper.

7

GAGE CONTINUED to hold his breath as Roxanne slid his belt buckle through the loops. She was a walking dream come true, but, dear Lord, he hadn't expected anything like this.

He dropped his head back as her hand caressed the hard length of him. Gripping the edges of the bench, he fought the urge to climax. She always aroused him with ease, but after the stress of the last day and a half, his body begged for release. His muscles clenched to the point of pain.

Then, she slid her hand to the base of his erection, and her mouth replaced her hands.

"Oh, hell."

He fought back a new, surging tide of arousal. He clamped his teeth together to keep his jaw from dropping. Roxanne didn't— Roxanne wouldn't—

Roxanne was.

Her agile tongue stroked him, her hot, wet mouth absorbed him. He fought desperately for control.

But he managed to keep his eyes open. No way was he missing the sight of her long dark hair—okay, admittedly, that was a little weird—bent over his lap, her hands kneading his thighs.

She dipped her tongue in the slit at the tip of his erection, and he moaned. He wasn't sure how much more he could handle, though a lifetime of her touch just might be long enough.

His climax surged through him before he could grasp another thought.

He tossed his head back and relished the explosion and release. He wanted to freeze-frame every moment with her, trying not to wonder if each one would be the last.

The pulses of satisfaction beat through him, draining his body and mind. His heart continued to race. He gasped for air, to find stability in the spinning world, finally slumping against the wall behind him.

After several silent moments passed, she lifted her head. "Are we ever going to do this in a bed again?"

"Are we ever going to do this at the same time?"

They shared a smile, then he leaned forward, cupping her face gently as he kissed her. "You're incredible."

Her face flushed. "I, uh… Well, I've never done that before. I was okay?"

Immeasurably touched, he drew her into his arms. "The best."

"I'm not doing a very good job of following my own rules," she said against his chest.

"I was never much for rules myself."

She threaded her fingers through his hair, wrapping his ponytail around her index finger. Despite the fact that they were in the dressing room of a tacky lingerie shop, she seemed disinclined to move. "Do you think this—" he assumed she meant the disguise "—is changing us?"

After years of undercover work, he'd wondered the same thing countless times. And, sometimes, he could no longer remember where the deception ended and he began. Was he corrupting Roxanne? Was he changing her? He didn't think he wanted to, but neither could he deny how much he was enjoying the commanding, adventurous woman she'd become since this whole mess started.

"Do you think you've changed?" he asked, disturbed by his thoughts.

"Yes," she said quickly, still staring at the ponytail, her fingers stroking its length. Then her green gaze connected with his. "I'm not as intimidated by you as I was before."

His heart gave him a good swift kick in the ribs for that. "I intimidated you?"

"I never could figure out what you were doing with *me*."

"*What?*"

"You could have any woman—"

He laid his finger over her lips. "Don't say that again. Dammit, R—" He stopped, just remembering in time not to use her real name. "You're the greatest, purest thing in my life," he said, gripping her shoulders, keeping his voice quiet. "I *don't want, will never* want anyone else."

"Then why did you lie to me?"

He closed his eyes, the hurt and accusation in her eyes too much to deal with. He finally opened them again, forcing himself to meet her gaze. "I was trying to protect you."

"Would you ever have told me?"

He hadn't really thought that far ahead. He'd been so sure he could keep both his lives separate. But she deserved his honesty now. "I don't know."

Her eyes angry, she pressed her lips together. "Will you do me a favor?"

"I'll try."

"No more lies. From this moment on, whatever happens, you'll tell me the truth."

In his business, making a pledge like that was impossible. He couldn't betray Treasury Department confidences. He couldn't always tell her where he was, or where he would be, or what he'd be doing. But he also realized she was challenging him, testing him. *Me or the job. Which is more important?*

He didn't like the thought of having his back against the wall, and he certainly didn't know if he could keep his promise, but he made it anyway. "The truth, from now on."

She slid her arms around his waist, hugging him tight. "Thank you."

"Uh, 'scuse me, Mr. Tailor?" a voice called from the other side of the curtain.

Gage sighed. *The real world intrudes.* "Yes?"

"Are you ready to buy now?"

Gage rearranged his clothing and stood, finding his knees still a bit unsteady, while Roxanne changed back into her clothes. Oddly enough, he felt as if they'd turned a corner. Though where it would lead, or when the next sharp curve would suddenly appear, he had no idea.

He bought the silver outfit. Hell, he was thinking of having the thing bronzed.

When he handed the clerk a pair of twenties, the man held them up to the light, one by one, then placed them under a magnifying glass. Though most stores these days made random counterfeit checks, the procedure set Gage's nerves on edge. "Problem?"

The man leaned forward. "My brother-in-law, he manages one of those big electronics superstore places in Metairie. He called me last night. Know what he found when they counted the cash box last night?" He glanced around briefly, then whispered, "Six hundred and forty dollars in funny money."

A sharp left suddenly hovered on the horizon.

"You MIGHT WANT to check those connections, sir. They're looking weak from this end."

From her seat on the park bench, Roxanne watched Gage pace by her for at least the tenth time, his cell phone plastered next to his ear. To say he was royally ticked off was an extreme understatement.

"Right. But a guy selling feather boas knows before I do. What's their excuse for *that?*"

Roxanne had no clue who he was talking to—some fellow agent, or maybe a superior, since he kept saying "sir." Earlier, she'd debated the wisdom of having this particular conversation in the middle of a public park, with Andrew Jackson staring down at them and dozens of tourists gaping at and photographing everything in sight. And using a cell phone, which supposedly any radio buff could tap into. Gage had simply snapped, "It's secure."

She hadn't said a word since.

Lord, the man was moody. She'd never seen this aspect in him. Around her, he'd always been calm and controlled. Another aspect of Dark Side Gage, she supposed.

Have to take the good with the bad, Rox.

And the sex in the lingerie dressing room had been *great*.

Though technically, even according to a former president, they hadn't had sex. But no sex hadn't been her self-imposed rule. She'd wanted no physical contact. And wisely, too. When she got her hands on the man, it wasn't just to give him a friendly hug.

She searched her resolve to break up with him, and even found that wavering. Logically, unemotionally she knew she couldn't stay with him. But, boy, did her body want to go out with a bang.

And her heart? She sighed. *Quietly breaking in half.*

"No," Gage said into the phone. "I've got plans for later."

Noting his careful choice of words, Roxanne wondered how much she figured into his plans. Annoying sidekick? Necessary distraction?

You're the greatest, purest thing in my life.

Not exactly a confession of undying love, but pretty darn close. And for the first time in her life, her resolve to keep her distance from law enforcement had wavered.

"Yes, sir. I'm out." He flipped the phone closed and sank onto the bench beside her. "Let's take a walk by the river."

He looked tired, so she grasped his hand in hers and left the park without saying a word. He walked with his head down, managing to look melancholy even in broad daylight amidst the partying crowds.

Strolling the riverfront sidewalk, she glanced up at him. "Who were you talking to?"

He drew a deep breath, then let the air escape slowly. "My father."

Her steps faltered. His boss. Somehow, in the middle of her own personal disaster, she'd forgotten his involvement.

"The electronics store had two fake hundred-dollar bills and a stack of twenty fake twenties when the cash drawer was counted at closing last night. They called NOPD. Some rookie detective drew the case, and he spent the better part of the night trying to solve the case on his own so he could be a big hero to the Feds." He shoved his hands into his pockets. "Idiot. And so, thanks to an eager beaver and bureaucratic red tape, the manager of Ooh, Ah knows more about my case than I do."

"Is Stephano behind this?"

"I can't imagine it's a coincidence."

Roxanne frowned. "He needed a CD player and some video games?"

"I'm sure the idea is to launder the money through the store. Whoever bought the merchandise with the counterfeit money will come back in a few days and return everything, getting a cash refund."

"Oh," she said, but her confusion deepened. "He's risking exposure over a few hundred bucks? That doesn't seem really smart."

Gage glanced down at her, admiration clearly reflected in his eyes. "Good call, Marina."

"And spending six hundred in cash...what if the sales clerk remembers him?"

"Another wrinkle."

They continued to walk along with the rest of the crowds, the Mississippi River chugging along beside them, bringing a brisk breeze. Roxanne puzzled through this odd turn in the investigation. "Stephano has to have other workers besides Mettles in on his plan for a job like this, right?"

"I would think so. He'd have to have a crew to cut the paper into bills, box it or bag it for transport."

"Whoever went shopping last night didn't go under Stephano's orders. He got greedy and slipped a few bucks into his own pocket."

Gage slid his arm around her waist, and a smile replaced the lines of frustration on his face. "That was pretty much my thought, as well."

"Really?"

"You make a pretty good detective. And don't slug me," he added before she could do just that.

"So what else did your—" Father? Boss? From Gage's strained and formal tone with the man, she didn't sense a normal father-son relationship, but one she found herself wildly curious about. "What else did he say?"

"You mean dear ol' dad? He thinks the cash last night is definitely connected to Stephano. And he also thinks Stephano is planning something much bigger than buying and returning a few stereos."

"So we all agree."

"He's also still furious I screwed up by involving you in this. He's threatening to pull me."

She stopped. Her gaze shot to his profile. "Off the case? That's ridiculous." Even as she felt a measure of guilt for causing him trouble, she couldn't believe his father would be so harsh. Or irresponsible. Gage was the only one who could get Stephano. "You've been working on it for six months. It's *your* case. We got a great lead today—that goon outside the lingerie store.

If he's there, something's going on in that property of Stephano's. Which one was it, by the way?''

Gage drew her off the path, where she was blocking the tides of people. "The florist's."

"Oh, that's kind of clichéd, don't you think?"

"I do."

"Anyway—" she waved her hands, getting into the spirit of untangling Stephano's plans, and showing that small-minded man who'd spawned a far superior son a thing or two about case solving "—we've got to get a peek inside that florist's. How about I create a distraction, while you—"

"I can get in there on my own, thank you. It's too dangerous for you."

She started to argue but knew that would get her nowhere, so she settled for silently plotting a way to make sure she was included in the adventure. The fact that she considered breaking into a mobster's lair an *adventure* wasn't lost on her. Changed? Good grief, she'd turned herself inside out.

"Mmm," she said neutrally. "Well, anyway, once it's confirmed that's where the equipment is, then we have to put our energies into figuring out how Stephano is going to make big bucks with his fake money. He's not going to buy a bunch of stuff. So...where do you go and drop a lot of money you can somehow exchange later without attracting too much attention?"

Even as the words were out of her mouth, she glanced toward the water. At the riverboats floating just feet offshore.

"A casino." Pleased with herself, she snapped her fingers. "He'd have to somehow be in league with the owners, of course. Heck, maybe he owns half these boats. But that could be it. He could funnel tons of cash through a casino. That's how Las Vegas was built over sixty years ago."

"He's always been a traditional kind of guy."

"I think we're on to something here. We'll have this case closed by Sunday, lock Stephano in the federal pen, you'll get a commendation from the President, *then* we'll see what 'dear ol' dad' thinks about *that*."

Suddenly, he cupped her face in his hands. "You keep this up, I'm going to begin to think you care."

She glanced away. Gage was too perceptive, and she couldn't let her heart get in the way of the work that had to be done, the decisions that had to be made. "Of course I do." She grinned to push back her worries. "Do I get a special commendation medal out of this?"

He stroked her cheek with the pad of his thumb. "I'll see what I can do."

The tenderness and laughter in his eyes made her sigh. Here was the charming man she'd fallen for so hard, so fast. Whose barest touch sent a delicious thrill racing through her blood. Whose light and dark sides surrounded her, both overwhelming and exciting her.

When he leaned forward and kissed her, his lips moving over hers with warmth and confidence, she slid her arms around his waist and held on.

"We should head back," he said quietly when he pulled away.

She and Gage alone in that sumptuous hotel room? Oh, no. *Bad* idea.

She grabbed his hand and tugged him back toward

the Quarter. "Sorry, sweetie, you promised shopping."

He simply looked heavenward.

ROXANNE DROPPED her bags just inside the door. "Oh, what a day!"

Gage raised his eyebrows at her fake, cheerful tone and dropped his wallet and room key on the entryway table.

She bobbed her head rapidly in the direction of the living area. "But you were so generous, baby." She made kissing noises.

Gage crossed to her, laying the back of his hand against his forehead.

"What are you doing?" she whispered.

"Checking for fever."

She batted his hand away. "What about, you know, the—" She mouthed, "Bugs."

"I made sure one of our people posing on the housekeeping staff cleaned the room while we were gone."

"You have people on the housekeeping staff?" Before today, this operation had seemed like Gage's one-man show, but now she'd gotten a better idea of its scope. There were agents checking out Stephano's properties, others following him and Mettles, and many others working on research. With his father running the show. Threatening him, telling him he'd screwed up. Because of her.

She flopped onto the sofa and concentrated on her and Gage's conversation. "Why didn't these people check the room yesterday?"

"Having housekeeping cleaning the room at ten

o'clock at night would have looked a little strange, don't you think?"

"Oh, right." She pulled off her new sandals, wincing a bit as she flexed her feet.

No wonder the first thing her dad always did when he came home from work was drop into his recliner. This cop business was tough on the bod.

"I need to check in," Gage said, kissing the top of her head as he'd done countless nights in their house before disappearing into his office to work.

She didn't call attention to his actions. She simply watched him walk across the room to the desk. And she wondered. About the case. About him and her.

After today, realizing the number of people involved in this case and the impact on the community, she felt a little selfish for her complaints on the subject of law enforcement. Even though she hadn't shown it often, she'd always known her father, brother and sister made an invaluable contribution to the public. Maybe, instead of resenting the consequences of the choices they made, she should have been thanking them.

What would Mother do? How would she feel if I'd been taken instead of her?

She would wonder who would go after scumbags like Stephano if people like Gage didn't sacrifice so much of their lives.

But she wasn't her mother. She couldn't live the life her mother had. She didn't have the strength.

Law enforcement needed Gage, and she needed peace. No matter how well matched they were in their passion and companionship, they didn't belong together. The scene in the dressing room hadn't changed anything. The next time she let her feelings for him sweep her into his arms—which she had no doubt would happen—nothing would change. They were still at an impasse.

When this weekend was over, the case closed, she'd still have to find the will to leave him.

Shoulders slumping, she focused on their afternoon. Despite the tension underlying their time together, she'd enjoyed shopping with him. Parading sexy clothes, elegant clothes, expensive clothes before him had been liberating and fun. She'd never been so conscious of her body and its effect on the male species until Gage. And seeing his seductive smile as she twirled by him in a skirt way shorter than anything she would have considered before this weekend was a moment she'd always hold near her heart.

She'd even bought something to wear to the casinos later that didn't make her feel weird and out of place. A gold lace pantsuit. Lying back on the sofa, the headrest supporting her neck, she recalled the stunned look on Gage's face as she'd exited the dressing room. The way his eyes had lit, considered and measured— and found her dazzling.

Though all the appropriate parts were covered by lining under the lace, the pants fit tight through her butt and thighs, then flared toward her feet. The shirt had a wide neckline, exposing her shoulders, and had lining only over her breasts, leaving her stomach peeking through the lacy pattern. She'd chosen designer gold stilettos to go with the outfit and had looked in the mirror in the dressing room and thought *I actually look as if I belong with him.*

Him, the supersuccessful investment banker.

She jerked to a sitting position, staring over the sofa at Gage as he typed on his laptop. "You can't afford those shoes on a cop's pay."

He glanced at her over his shoulder. "Well, I have a bit more than my salary in the bank. My grandparents left me some money."

"You can't use that for my shoes."

"They left me four million, Rox."

"Oh." She lay back down. Then sat up. "Hell, Gage. Four *million?*"

He just grinned, then turned back to his computer.

Roxanne found she couldn't lie still any longer, so she strode to the bathroom to shower. Afterward, tucked into a plush hotel bathrobe, she strolled back into the living area and found Gage locking his briefcase. "We need to go play leisure-loving mob conspirators again."

"Where?" If she had to walk another block, even in her snazzy new sandals, she was balking.

"How about the pool?"

She smiled. "How about I get the sunscreen?"

HE WAS MAKING progress.

Roxanne's determination to leave him was wavering.

Stretched beside her in a lounge chair by the hotel pool, Gage took advantage of his sunglasses to stare shamelessly at her body and consider her mind.

Since she wore a candy-apple red bikini, he had to work hard at the mental part.

She hadn't liked his father's heavy-handed motivation tactics, so he hadn't told her his boss had threatened to pull him off every case at some point. Dad was a by-the-book guy, and he was constantly baffled by the rebellious son he'd brought into the business. It was an old conflict he didn't expect ever to fully reconcile, and he'd long ago made his peace with that reality.

But knowing Roxanne had forced him to acknowledge that his relationship with his father had shaped his other relationships. Raised by a distant, sometimes hard man had turned him into a loner, unsure with tender feelings. He knew Roxanne needed more from him emotionally. He just didn't know how to put his feelings for her into words.

Tell her you love her, you dummy.

The last woman he'd loved—his mother—hadn't stuck around when he'd poured out his heart. What if Roxanne still rejected him? Love or not, hadn't she just told him this morning she didn't want the man he was? The cop. The loner.

She laid her hand on his bare thigh, and he nearly jumped out of his skin. "Baby, could you—" She stopped, angling her head. "Where'd you go?"

He picked up her hand and kissed her palm. "I'm here."

Since she also wore dark sunglasses, he couldn't discern her reaction to his touch, but hoped her heart was hammering as quickly as his. "Pretending" to flirt with Roxanne was the kind of undercover work he'd could get into.

"I just wanted another bottle of water. I'm roasting out here."

He slid one finger down her tanned leg. "You're glistening. It's sexy."

"It's sweat."

"I think you need some more sunscreen."

She peeked at him over the rims of her sunglasses. "Oh, but where would I find a volunteer to apply it?"

He laughed, walking his fingers up her thigh. "I wonder."

She captured his hand before he could reach her hip. "Water."

Reluctantly, he rose. As he walked across the pool deck toward the bar, he took the opportunity to again check out a pair of Stephano's goons, sitting at a table shaded by a bright yellow umbrella. They had on Hawaiian-print shirts, dark bathing suits and deck shoes to set off their glowing white legs. They looked like a couple of tourists from Jersey. Which was the idea, he guessed.

The one on the left was the guy he'd seen coming out of the florist's earlier. A minor leg breaker in Stephano's organization named Vince, he'd learned from his computer research. And his instincts to be visible today had been right on the money. They'd report back to their boss about shopping, relaxing by the pool and, later, casino hopping. All in keeping with his image, and hopefully settling any nerves set off by Roxanne's unexpected appearance at the bar last night.

He retrieved the water, then headed back to Roxanne, struck stupid again by the sight of her long, slender legs, her breasts spilling from the top of her revealing bikini. *Oh, my, duty calls. It's a tough job...*

He leaned over and kissed her as he handed her the bottle of water—hey, they had to keep up appearances, right? "Anything else I can do for you?" he asked huskily when he pulled back.

She laid her hand against his bare chest, and, if he wasn't mistaken, let her gaze rove leisurely over his body. "Wear a turtleneck."

He stroked the soft skin between her breasts. "Same goes."

She groaned. "This is harder than I thought."

He raised his eyebrows. He could definitely relate.

"That's not what I meant," she said primly, though she slid her hand across the top of his shoulder. "Pretending," she whispered.

"Who's pretending? I want you. I always want you."

Her throat moved as she swallowed. "I want you, too, but—"

He pressed his lips to hers again. "Let's just leave it at that." He dropped into his chair before she justified or explained her desires. If this was the pretend world, he'd reside here happily the rest of his life.

But after another half hour of teasing, touching and flirting, he was on the verge of screaming. Every brush of her fingers or glimpse of her smile had his erection swelling, his muscles contracting.

"I'm turning over," Roxanne announced suddenly, dropping the back of her lounge chair and flipping over onto her stomach.

Thank God. If he watched one more bead of sweat disappear between her breasts, he was going to lose it.

She extended the bottle of sunscreen. "Could you rub some lotion on my back?"

Gage glanced from the bottle to the slope of Roxanne's tanned, bare back, the scrap of red material covering her backside, the length of her legs. His erection pulsed.

She waggled the bottle. "Come on, Gage."

He grabbed the bottle and swallowed hard as he sat on the edge of her chair, his hip brushing her side. Letting the lotion dribble onto her skin, he licked his lips, then set the bottle aside and flexed his fingers. *It's a tough job...*

As he rubbed the lotion over her shoulders, he bit back a groan. Warmed by the sun, dampened by sweat, her skin felt like silk.

"Mmm," she moaned.

Sweat rolled down his face. He massaged the slippery lotion down her spine, feeling her muscles bunch and release, her breathing quickening. His hand nearly spanned her waist, and the sight of the two dimples just above her butt was beyond erotic. He couldn't resist sliding his fingertips beneath the edge of her bikini bottoms.

Her breath caught as he caressed the top slope of her backside. Knowing that dozens of people, in addition to the mob, surrounded them lent a forbidden thrill to his touch.

But she didn't push his hand away. She lay still as a statue, her hands gripping the chair's edge. Her knuckles were white.

Smiling, he trailed his fingers across the slick material of the bathing suit. He smoothed lotion on her legs, lingering on the inner curve of her thigh. When he brushed the heat between her legs, she twitched. Further encouraged, he worked one finger beneath the elastic of the suit, finding her damp, hot, aroused. He moved his finger up, then down, then up again, reveling in the way her body quivered, as if asking for more.

Hiding his explorations, he leaned over her, brushing her hair away from her neck. "Comfy, darling?" he whispered in her ear.

"You're making me crazy," she said breathlessly.

"I'm so glad I'm not alone."

He placed a kiss beneath her ear as he gently pushed his finger deep inside her body.

She gasped. "Gage, please."

In pain himself, he shifted, deciding they'd hung out at the pool long enough. If he didn't get Roxanne naked and horizontal and in a bed, he was going to—

"Damn."

As he stilled his hands, Roxanne tensed. "Gage?"

He glared at the waitress serving the elderly couple across from them. "We've got a problem with a waitress."

Roxanne lifted her head. He had no doubt she was glaring at him from behind her sunglasses. "What are you talking about?"

He turned her head to the right.

"That's no waitress. That's Toni."

8

ROXANNE WAS ABSOLUTELY going to shoot that woman.

Clear as day, clad in her white-blond wig and a pool-waitress uniform, talking to an elderly couple, stood Toni. Nerve endings that had been primed for lovemaking fizzled. Anger took the edge off her arousal. Gage moved his hand.

All in all, the mood was *completely* ruined.

"What does she think she's doing?"

"Causing trouble—as usual."

"Where did she get that waitress uniform?"

"I don't want to know." He patted her leg. "Come on. We need to go before she does something ridiculous."

"You mean something *besides* stalking us?"

He wrapped a towel around his waist and scooped up the sunscreen. "Besides that."

How could he sound so calm? Roxanne felt as if her heart was going to jump onto the pool deck. Gage had told her Stephano's men were hanging around, but he hadn't said where. She'd been glad. She didn't want to get caught staring. But now her *former* best friend could blow their cover—and possibly get them all killed—with a wrong word or two.

Gage slid his arm around her waist as they strolled—though Roxanne felt like running—across the pool deck and toward the entrance to the hotel. She indulged in another moment of ogling the man next to her. Sleek muscles, tanned skin sprinkled with black hair and the confident, controlled way he moved all rolled into one irresistible package.

She sure hadn't been resisting.

And the desire flowing through her body still pulsed just beneath the surface of her fake calm, waiting to spring, fighting for release.

When they stopped in front of the elevators, a familiar voice from behind them said, "I'm watching you."

Thankfully, the hallway was deserted, but who knew when Stephano's goons would show up? "Go away," Roxanne whispered to her friend.

"You two are hiding something."

Roxanne whirled. "Who could with you around?"

Toni simply sashayed toward the door, her trim butt swaying in the tight blue shorts of her uniform. "I won't abandon you."

Even as Roxanne sighed over Toni's persistence, she couldn't help smiling. A more loyal friend she'd never find. And at least Toni wasn't mad anymore. She was just really in the way.

As the elevator doors opened, Roxanne said quietly to Gage, "She thinks she's protecting me."

"As long as she keeps out of my way."

He was annoyed. Well, she could hardly blame him. Toni could blow this case in a big way. The silence grew uncomfortable on the ride up to their room. Roxanne bit her lip, not knowing how to get his mood back on the romantic side. If she had to spend the night trolling casinos, she wanted to at least be able to pretend they were on a date and enjoy Gage's attention and company.

He pushed open the door, then let her precede him inside.

"I'm sorry, Gage. She doesn't mean—"

The next thing she knew, her back was flat against the door, with Gage's hot mouth pressed to hers.

She thrust her arms around his neck, pressing her aching breasts against his warm, bare chest. Oh, God, it felt good to be close to him. He pinned her against the wall with his hips, and she had no doubt he'd managed to set aside his frustration at Toni and maintain the desire started at the pool. His erection, pressed against her stomach, sending her head spiraling.

His tongue tangled with hers. He grabbed a handful of her hair as he kissed her, holding her head at the angle he wanted, making sure escape wasn't an option.

She had no intention of going anywhere unless he was with her.

She poured all the desire, frustration and need of the last several hours into her kiss. She wanted him to want her above all else, beyond reason and thought, until she was the only thing in his life, heart or soul.

He jerked back suddenly and, breathing heavily, he stared at her. With his sunglasses on he looked dark and dangerous. Her heart hammered, her blood pulsed. But, wanting to see his eyes, she pulled his glasses off.

Regret shined back at her.

Oh, no, you don't. She stalked forward, even as he retreated.

"Rox, I lost it." He tunneled his hand through his hair. "I don't know what—"

She planted her mouth over his, clutching the back of his neck as she kissed him and held him to her. "Do you know how much I want you right now?" she asked against his lips.

Then, she bit him.

He jolted back in shock, then wrapped his arms around her. "I got the idea."

She kissed his throat, savoring the rapid pulse beating beneath her lips.

Cupping her backside, he pulled her tight against his erection. "Ah, better."

As she tried to catch her breath, she squirmed. "Not enough."

He hooked his thumbs around the waistband of her bikini bottoms, yanking them down. She kicked them off even as his towel dropped and she tugged down his swim trunks, wrapping her hands around the hard length of him.

Sucking in a breath, he dropped his head back and closed his eyes. "Oh, man."

The need for completion wracked her insides, but she was so enthralled with the pleasure clearly swamping him that she simply stared, her hands trembling as she stroked him.

Then he lowered his head. His gaze met hers.

The heat in his brown eyes and the tossed strands of his ponytail threw her for a second. He was her same old lover, yet he wasn't. Two sides of a complicated man. Maybe life wasn't as simple as she had tried to make it. Gage was more than she thought. *She* was more than she thought. Love was more than she thought.

He kissed her fiercely as he lifted her above his erection, pressing her back against the wall, then buried himself deep inside her body.

She gasped.

Had it been forever since she'd been a part of him? Since she'd felt this pulsing fullness and hunger, needing him with desperation, knowing she could really only possess him until his own desire was sated.

He lifted her, then lowered her again, and she held on tightly to his neck, wrapped her legs around his hips, her back leveraged against the hard wall. His strength and power and control seduced her. She'd been pulsing on the edge of satisfaction since he'd first touched her by the pool, and now it took very little movement to coil her tighter, bringing her higher and closer to her climax.

"Gage," she moaned as he pressed deeper inside, withdrawing and thrusting quickly, as if he, too, was caught in the roaring tide.

Her breath hitched suddenly as the peak came. The pleasure shuddered into spasms, then blossomed and spread. She dropped her head on his shoulder, bracing herself as he drove into her one last time, his own climax taking over his movements.

As her sweat-slicked thighs slid from his hips, she wondered how she'd ever let him go.

GAGE BRACED his arm against the wall and his body against Roxanne. "We didn't make it to the bed."

Her breath still coming in spurts, she leaned drunkenly against his chest. "Nope."

She tried to stand straight, but wobbled, so he wrapped his arm around her waist. She still wore her bikini top and her wig was crooked, but she had a sated smile on her face.

He pulled the wig off, and strands of her own dark red hair tumbled free. "That thing must be hot," he said, tossing the hairpiece on the sofa.

"A bit. Thanks."

He searched his feelings for regret and could find none. He'd lost all semblance of control and finesse, but he didn't care. He'd made her happy, put that sappy grin on her face, that flush on her cheeks. He wouldn't let her leave him. No matter what he had to do.

Digging for strength, he straightened his swimsuit, then scooped her into his arms, carrying her into the bedroom. They had a few hours before they had to head to the casinos, and he wasn't wasting a minute.

He kissed her lips softly and laid her on the bed. "You want anything?"

Smiling, she drew her hand down his chest. "What are you offering?"

He'd captured her hand, pressing his lips to her palm. "Something to drink...for the moment. Later, anything you want."

"Mmm." She kissed the base of his throat, and his pulse leaped. "In that case, water would be great."

Reluctantly, he left her, walking into the living area to grab a bottle of water from the minifridge. Need for her touch still hovered just beneath his calm surface, and for the first time in his life he considered chucking his duties and responsibilities. He could call his father, tell him to stuff his rules, his threats and his case, and take Roxanne away from all of this.

When they took down Stephano, another scumbag would just rise up to take his place. Nothing ever seemed to change. But as he turned the bottle up and drank, he rejected the idea before it took root. He had to see this case through. After Stephano was behind bars, he wasn't making any promises to the department, but until then he'd make the necessary sacrifices. He was sure of very little these days; he couldn't lose his honor, too.

When he returned to the bedroom, she was lying on her side, completely nude.

He halted in the doorway, momentarily struck by her simple beauty. When she smiled and crooked her finger, he went to her, of course, holding out the water bottle, trying desperately to get a manageable hold on his desire.

She lifted up on her forearm and drank, her gaze fixed on his face. She looked confident and sexy. The combination was different than he was used to from her, but intoxicating nonetheless. His betrayal had hurt her, he knew, but he wondered if this whole mess had also made her stronger. It had certainly drawn them closer together. Until this weekend, he hadn't realized her deep insecurities regarding him. It was almost funny that while she hadn't known what he saw in her, he'd wondered what he'd ever done to deserve someone like her. Before, he'd thought quiet shyness was dominant in her personality, but she'd revealed a bold, self-possessed side that intrigued him even more. He was falling for her all over again.

With the tip of his finger, he drew a gliding line

down her side, from the tip of her shoulder to the curve of her waist and down her thigh and calf. "You are so beautiful," he said huskily.

She blinked, then her eyes went sly. "Yeah? You're kind of beautiful yourself." She tugged him down by the string on his bathing suit. "But you're over-dressed."

He knelt at the end of the bed and took the water from her hand, setting the bottle on the floor. Then he slid his hand across her silky stomach. "What did you have in mind?"

She reached out and grabbed his ponytail, lazily threading her fingers through the long strands. "Making love until we pass out."

He brushed aside her hair and kissed her neck, in-haling the spicy, sensual perfume he'd bought her ear-lier and the womanly scent that belonged only to Rox-anne. "I could go for that." When she continued to play with his ponytail, he added, "I think you like that thing."

"Maybe you should grow one."

He stilled briefly, wondering if she'd be around long enough to see his hair grow. Not wanting to break her relaxed mood, he continued trailing kisses down her throat. "Maybe I will."

He moved down, over the slope of her breast. He flicked out his tongue as he drew circles across her skin, drawing closer and closer to the nipple. Her breathing quickened. One hand clenched his bicep. When he sucked her nipple into his mouth, her back arched off the mattress.

The leisurely pace, the subdued lighting of the hotel room in the middle of the day, reminded him of a weekend they'd spent at a bed-and-breakfast in the mountains of North Carolina. They'd barely left the room, except to explore the woodsy trails surrounding the property. Room service, music, slow dancing, wine and sex had been the order of the day. He wanted more days and nights like that. Carbon copies, variations, new inventions. He wanted it all. With her. He just needed to figure out *how*.

As he lavished attention on her breasts with his mouth, he trailed his hand down her stomach, dipping between her legs. Wet heat surrounded his fingers. He stroked her rhythmically as she gasped for air, as she clutched the bedspread, as she tightened her muscles.

His own body hardened and throbbed. He so enjoyed exciting her.

Then he remembered the champagne.

The weekend of the bed-and-breakfast, they'd drank champagne after dinner, most of the bottle winding up on them instead of in them. He wanted, *needed* to remind her of those simpler times.

"Be right back," he said, placing a quick kiss on her stomach.

"What?" She raised her head, no doubt glaring at him as he darted from the room.

Heart racing, he retrieved a mini bottle of champagne from the fridge. He popped the cork as the walked through the bedroom doorway.

Her eyes widened. "What's *that* for?"

He drank a quick sip from the bottle, then held it out for her. She wrapped her hands around the bottle's neck, sipping, her gaze locked on his, though she still looked confused.

But when he took back the bottle and drizzled the champagne across her stomach, she sucked in a surprised breath, and her eyes lit with understanding.

He smeared the liquid down her side, dipping his finger in her navel, then licking the effervescence from her skin.

She moaned, dropping her head back, burying her hands in his hair.

Smiling against her stomach, he drew his tongue in a circle, starting in the center of her belly button, slowly widening the arc, until he'd scraped the undersides of her breasts, then the hair at the juncture of her thighs. Where he poured more champagne and drank from the wet heat of her body.

Her hips came off the mattress. Silently begging him for more.

More champagne accompanied his journey down her inner thigh, behind her knee, across her ankle, between her toes.

When he rose to start at her other hip, she jerked upward, grabbing the waistband of his bathing suit, twisting the fabric in her fist. "You start on the other side, we're gonna have words."

He smiled, nibbled her lips then drizzled champagne down her chest.

She flinched, releasing him. "Gage, please."

He lapped up the drink dripping off her breast. "Mmm. I like the sound of that."

She flopped back on the bed.

He teased each nipple to hardness with his mouth, then slid his tongue down her opposite side. He was careful to avoid the one spot he sensed she needed the most attention. She thrashed and moaned. His erection swelled and throbbed.

When he was certain he'd die if he didn't get inside her, he shucked his bathing suit and set aside the bottle, poising himself between her thighs. He rubbed the entrance to her body with his hardness, and she wrapped her legs around his waist, her eyes popping open, her gaze connecting with his.

Swamped with hunger and tenderness, he thrust forward. Her liquid heat surrounded him, shooting his need higher. He had to grit his teeth to keep from climaxing.

Then he moved. Had to. His body had taken control now, and there was no holding back. He slid in, then out, fighting to stay in control, draw out the intense pleasure. He tried to increase the rhythm gradually, but he couldn't keep control. Climax was chasing him, urging him.

Their gazes met, Roxanne clutching his arms as she reached her peak, her body pumping his erection. The pleasure on her face bringing about his own. He exploded. Satisfaction rolled through his senses, sweat rolled down his back. He collapsed on top of her, his breath heaving.

Weakly, Roxanne patted his shoulder. "There better be more champagne in that bottle, baby, 'cause it's my turn now."

HER BODY STILL echoing from her last orgasm, Roxanne drew slow circles across Gage's damp, sticky chest. "We need a shower."

He moaned. "I need vitamins first."

She lightly slapped his shoulder. "I mean a real

shower." Experimentally, she moved her legs. Tight muscles and tacky calves. "I don't remember the champagne being this sticky before."

"We wound up in the hot tub before."

Her face heated as she recalled the decadent abandon of that whole weekend. "Right."

He stroked her hair, and her eyes drooped with the languid, comforting movement. What she was doing in this bed, indulging in passion with a man she'd just broken up with that morning, she had no idea. Probably making a big mistake. But she was too damn satisfied to worry about repercussions at the moment.

Practicality would hit her soon enough. Then the fantasy world would vanish.

Fighting off a sense of dread, she twined her leg around his. She breathed in the scent of his cologne, absorbed the warmth of his skin. She could definitely lounge here for the next hour or so. The next fifty years or so.

"Can you see the clock?" he asked.

Hello, reality. She glanced at the bedside clock. "It's six-thirty."

"How long will it take you to get ready?"

She sighed, seeing the prospects for her nap disappear. "To get all that hair and makeup back in place? At least an hour."

He patted her bare butt. "Playtime's over." He rolled off the bed, then padded across the room and retrieved a pair of jeans from the dresser drawer. Slipping them on, he said, "I'll call room service. You get in the shower."

Flopped on her stomach, she still managed to keep

her gaze glued to his very fine backside. "Since when do you wear jeans?"

Bare-chested, he turned, bracing his hands against the door frame. "I've always—" He stopped, his gaze shifting away. "Jeans didn't really fit for a financial adviser, I guess."

A hollow ache invaded her chest. She was beginning to hate reality. "Who are you, Gage?"

His gaze connected with hers. There was no mistaking the hurt and regret reflected in his dark brown eyes. "Hell if I know." Then he turned and strode into the other room.

Grumbling, Roxanne crawled off the bed. "What's *that* supposed to mean?"

Men were a real pain in the ass, she decided as she trudged into the bathroom. She showered with a loofah sponge, applied a fresh coat of tanning cream, then stood nude in front of the mirror to apply her makeup while the lotion dried.

Men. With their hard bodies, great butts, secrets and egos and dark sides. Heartache and frustration. That's all they were good for. And she had to go and pick the most hair-pulling one of all.

A cop. A *cop*, for heaven's sake. Dedicated to truth, justice and the American way. Even if he had to sacrifice himself in the process.

Actually, Rox, that's kind of noble.

"Ha!" she said, pointing a finger at her reflection. "That's just what he wants me to think, so I can admire him and appreciate him. Love him and—"

Accept him.

"Forget it."

But she refused to look herself in the eye as she said

the words. Quite a feat when one was applying eye-
liner.

Once the makeup was complete, she retrieved her
wig from the sofa, noting Gage sat—still bare-
chested—in front of his computer, and noting with
disgust that after a couple of shakes, the wig's curls
fell perfectly into place. Why couldn't her real hair
look like that?

Back in the bathroom, she pinned her hair back and
arranged the wig over her head. Then she wriggled
into her sexy gold top-and-pants set. As she slid her
foot into the jeweled, gold-trimmed stilettos, she
could no longer deny that her attempt at orneriness
was to ward off the excitement fluttering in her belly.
In a weird way she didn't want to examine too closely,
she was looking forward to tonight.

Prowling under the bright lights of the casinos,
skulking around a dark warehouse disguised as a florist—there was no way she was letting Gage handle
that alone—hanging proudly on Gage's arm throughout the whole process. It all seemed mysterious and
exciting. Would examining tax-law changes ever be
the same?

"Maybe," she hedged to her reflection, and the
stranger who stared back at her.

Two days ago, Roxanne had been perfectly happy
balancing revenue against expenses. Marina, how-
ever, wore clothes suited to *Playboy* bunnies and gave
blow jobs in dressing rooms. Two sides of the same
woman? Dark and light?

"Dinner's here, baby," Gage called from the other
room.

Roxanne fluffed her hair and pursed her red-tinted

lips. She really shouldn't have deep thoughts on an empty stomach.

But as she strode from the bathroom, the ideas wouldn't go away. Was she a hypocrite? Putting down Gage's job while she herself enjoyed participating in the work? The idea certainly made her uncomfortable.

Gage was next to the table, lifting a silver dome from a plate of pasta when she walked into the other room. "Good, you're—" Staring at her, he froze. "Ready," he finished softly.

She forced herself to put her hand on her hip and spin, wishing she didn't feel so ridiculously pleased that he couldn't take his eyes off her. "I look like I should be cavorting with Hugh Hefner at one of his pajama parties."

He extended his hand, which she took, then he assisted her into a chair at the table. "Hef should be so lucky." From behind her, he brushed aside her hair and placed a kiss on the side of her neck. "You're delicious."

She shivered and forced herself to stare at her plate. Shrimp and crawfish pasta. "Yum. *This* looks delicious."

"I know which one I'd rather have," he said as he walked around the table and took his place opposite her.

Still bare-chested.

Roxanne sighed, but dug into her pasta. The seafood was tossed with a creamy garlic sauce that was heavenly. The meal was so good she nearly, *nearly* managed to set aside her lust for the hunk of man across from her to enjoy it.

"So, what's the plan for tonight?" she asked as she leaned back and sipped her water.

"Your plan is to stick close to me, smile a lot and don't talk too much."

Her jaw dropped. "Gage, I want to help."

He glanced up. "You are."

"No, I mean really help. Like I did with figuring out how Stephano is laundering the money."

"Like we *think* he is. We could be way off base."

She crossed her arms over her chest. "But you don't think so."

"No." Sighing, he tossed his napkin on the table. "Rox, honey, this is dangerous. Leave the crime solving to the professionals."

"Rox, honey?" she repeated very quietly as he winced. She rose, leaning across the table and glaring at him. "Now, see here, *honey*. I had the same facts you did, probably even fewer, and came to the same conclusion you did, and nearly as quickly. You have ten years' experience doing this. I have—" she purposely glanced at her watch "—twenty-three hours. What does that tell you about how much help I can be?"

His eyes lit with desire. "Have I told you how sexy you are when you're angry?"

"A couple of times. Now, what should I do tonight?"

He stood, pacing away from the table. "We stick to the poker tables. I play...you watch. Pay special attention to the people who go to the window to buy chips and cash them in. Does anybody go often? Does it take the cashier a long time to hand over the cash—in other words, a long time to count back the winnings? If so, what kind of people are at the window during that transaction? The counterfeit money probably won't be passed to a member of the public. Like a guy from Des Moines in sandals and a yellow polo. It will be somebody shadier. Maybe a gambler. Someone desperate, who won't look too closely at the cash before passing it on."

"How does Stephano know who he's really passing money to? Look at us."

"He doesn't. But remember a pro can't completely hide who he is. It's in the eyes, the shrewdness, the calculated movements and careful words."

The sickness of betrayal rolled through her, realizing how perfectly he'd just described himself, and what a fool she'd been not to see it sooner. "You hid yourself well enough."

He stopped pacing, glancing at her, regret passing through his eyes.

"I'm sorry. Damn." How many times would she make him pay for his lies? "I didn't mean to bring that up. It just popped out. I—"

"It's okay." Pulling her into his arms, he rubbed her back. "I understand your anger."

She wanted to tell him she wasn't angry, not anymore, but since she wasn't entirely sure herself, she kept silent and just relished their embrace.

He leaned back and kissed her forehead. "I have something for you."

Ridiculously, her heart jolted. "A present for me?" They'd been together all day. When had he done that? she wondered as he strode into the bedroom.

He returned a few moments later and held out a small, rectangular black box.

Jewelry?

She stopped, her hands shaking as she realized what he'd done. The gesture was romantic and impulsive and sweet, and she wanted nothing to do with it. She didn't want a memento of their ruined future. She didn't even want to open the box. But, with tears stinging her eyes, she lifted the lid.

The diamond and emerald necklace she'd almost tried on earlier lay against a pillow of black velvet. The one that matched her engagement ring.

She wished she could pretend joy, but a veil of sadness fell over her as she gazed at the sparkling gems. She'd never again wear her ring, and reminding her of that reality cost her more emotionally than she was willing to give.

She forced her gaze to his. "It's beautiful, but I can't accept—"

He yanked the necklace from the case, fastening the clasp around her neck. "You can and you will." He straightened the chain, then spun her, his movements jerky. "Your disguise requires something gaudy."

It's not gaudy, she wanted to scream. *It's...beautiful.*

Instead, she silently looked into his cold, dark eyes and just felt miserable.

9

GAGE AVOIDED Roxanne's eyes and glared at the glittering stones resting against her throat.

She doesn't want your gifts.

She doesn't want you.

"I'm getting in the shower," he snapped, then stormed into the bedroom.

Nothing had changed. She'd share her body but not her life. To think he'd actually fantasized about sliding her engagement ring back on her finger. What a joke. He wasn't going to get her back. No matter how many times he brought her to the peak of passion. No matter how many compliments he gave her.

He stood under the showerhead, letting the water beat the back of his neck.

Maybe he belonged with the scum and the lawless. At least they were consistent. He didn't have any confusion about how to deal with them. They didn't make him consider giving up a lifetime of hard-won respect and a career that fulfilled him as nothing else ever had. They didn't make his heart ache and turn his insides to mush. They didn't make him long for places where he didn't belong. Home. Family. Peace.

Hell, she was just a woman. He could practically hear his colleagues' laughter ringing in his ears. Gage Dabon acting like an idiot over a woman. It was inconceivable. There were many more out there and plenty less complicated. He didn't need *her*. He didn't—

Damn. His throat tight, he slammed his fist against the tiled wall.

He was in love with her. All the way, head-over-heels, can't-imagine-his-life-without-her love.

And he was really pissed off about it.

THERE WAS NO POSSIBLE WAY she still loved him.

Roxanne sat in the raucous casino next to Gage, pretending to watch the poker game, while her mind spun in a complete panic. He'd lied to her—continually, daily. His job was the very definition of uncertainty and danger. He was moody and difficult and controlling.

She ordered her heart to stop dreaming. Immediately.

Ever since he'd draped that necklace around her, he'd barely spoken. Knowing their uncomfortable stalemate was for the best, she hadn't tried to pull him from his chilling anger.

In fact, she was starting to get pretty ticked off herself. She'd let him distract her with his body. She'd succumbed to memories and passion. But she wasn't forgetting her role in his life was extremely temporary. She wanted to go back to her tidy house, her stable business, her organized files and put all this intrigue and adventure behind her.

And by damn that's exactly what she was going to do.

SETTING HIS burning cigarette in an ashtray, Gage glanced at the cards in his hand—a king-high straight.

Great. He'd make a fortune while he lost the only thing that really mattered.

He nearly smiled at the irony.

Put it aside, agent. Bad guys are lurking, remember?

As he tossed a few more chips on the pile, he glanced around the room, noting the various tables of poker players, the roulette wheels, craps tables and endless lights and bells of the slots. This was the second riverboat casino they'd visited, and he'd seen nothing. None of Stephano's goons. No cashiers with shifty eyes or odd behavior. Tourists and local young people were thick as molasses. And he hadn't spotted a single professional cardsharp.

The only moment he couldn't set aside occurred an hour ago when a young couple from Kansas had won a big slot payoff. A smooth pit boss had escorted them to the cashier and personally supervised the payout. The boss was young—late twenties, early thirties—blond, slickly handsome and well dressed, but something about his charming smile had set Gage's senses on alert. Like the guy was trying too hard.

Or maybe I'm just trying too hard.

Gage's straight won the pot, earning him a few cheers and a hearty pat on the back from the Stetson-wearing cowboy next to him. He dropped a pile of chips into Roxanne's palm. "Why don't you go cash these in, baby."

She set down her glass of champagne and forced a smile he knew she didn't feel. "Sure thing, honey."

How could giving the woman an expensive necklace piss her off so much? he wondered as he watched her walk toward the cashier. Of course, it wasn't the necklace so much as the meaning behind the jewelry and the man who'd given it to her, and wow, her butt was spectacular in those tight lacy pants.

As he forced his attention back to the game, the same smooth pit boss Gage had noticed earlier fell into step beside Roxanne. Gage tensed, but he resisted the urge to interfere. She was barely twenty feet away, and the escort was no doubt casino policy—to protect their clients from pickpockets and keep management aware of high and frequent payouts. But as the dealer tossed out his new hand, Gage couldn't make his fingers relax.

The guy leaned close to Roxanne as she said something, then laughed. A flash of light winked.

What the hell...?

Gage laid down his initial bet, but he studied the boss's profile. There was definitely something familiar. And if the guy moved another millimeter closer to Roxanne, he was going to lose a lot of his familiar parts.

"Hey, slick, you with us?" the cowboy next to him asked.

Gage pulled his attention back to the game, noting with dismay he'd bet heavily and didn't have crap. Shrugging, he tossed a couple more chips into the pile—maybe nobody else had anything—and continued to watch Roxanne and the boss approach one of the payout windows.

He could only see the cashier—a young, attractive woman with medium-brown hair—from the waist up, but he could see her smile and snap to attention at the appearance of the pit boss. The boss gestured to Roxanne's chips, which she slid through the opening under the glass window. The cashier stacked the chips quickly, then disappeared, returning moments later with a handful of cash. During all this, the pit boss leaned casually against the wall, smiling and talking with Roxanne.

Flirting with her, in his expert opinion.

Gage kept his jaw clenched and his temper on hold as the cash was counted and slipped into an envelope, which Roxanne folded and dropped in her purse. Then the boss escorted her back to the table where Gage sat.

"If there's anything further I can do, miss, just let me know," he said, barely glancing at Gage as he walked away.

As Roxanne slid onto her stool, Gage laid his hand over hers. "Missed you, babe." And since there were some advantages to being in charge and in public, he kissed her cheek, inhaling her perfume and absorbing the silkiness of her skin. "Let's go after this hand."

She gripped his fingers hard, though she seemed relaxed when she said, "I could use some fresh air."

Fresh air. Their signal that they needed to talk privately. Gage laid down his hand with the rest, noting the cowboy won easily with three-of-a-kind.

He wrapped his arm protectively around her as they slipped through the doorway and into the humid night. Nuzzling her neck, he guided her along the upper deck toward the railing, hoping they looked like a couple wrapped up only in each other.

Wasn't pretending fun?

He retrieved his silver cigarette case and lit one, blowing the smoke toward the river churning below them.

"Do you have to smoke that?" she asked, her voice low and annoyed.

"Yes." He braced one arm against the railing and kept one around her waist, holding her tight against his body. All he needed now was her trying to bolt. "What's with Blondie?"

"Who?"

"The pit boss."

"Oh, it's not him." She paused, considering. "Well, maybe it is. Anyway, when he and I walked up to the window, the cashier counted my chips like the other casino did, but then she opened a safe sitting on the floor and gave me the cash from there."

He remembered the cashier disappearing for a few moments. At least that could be explained. "She gave you a couple grand, right? Maybe she just didn't want to deplete the cash box."

She shook her head. "I don't think so. That old lady ahead of me told everybody she won five thousand, and the cashier went straight to the drawer and the cash. She had to kneel to get to the safe. I would have noticed her doing that with the old lady."

"Maybe she did, and you missed it."

"My job was observation. She didn't go to the safe."

Frankly, he couldn't remember, so he kept silent and admired her attention to detail. That accounting background, he supposed. He flicked ash from his cigarette. "Did the pit boss go with the old lady?"

"No. The only ones I saw him with before was the couple from Kansas."

"And did the cashier go straight to the drawer that time?"

"No." She smiled. "She disappeared for a few seconds. I'm on to something, aren't I?"

"It would seem so. Pit boss equals a disappearing cashier." He pretended to inhale from the cigarette, blowing the majority of the smoke out instead of into his lungs—he hoped. This damn job was going to give him cancer as well as an ulcer and heartache. Then he remembered the flash. What had that been about? "Did he have any unusual characteristics?"

Roxanne's vivid green eyes glowed beneath the moonlight. "As a matter of fact, he did. It's hard to see unless he smiles really big, but he has a diamond stud imbedded in one of his eye teeth."

Gage's pulse skipped a beat.

"You know him, don't you?"

"I know who he is, yes."

"Who?"

"Stephano's nephew."

"No kidding?" she asked, her eyes wide.

"No kidding. The hair threw me. The last picture we have of him, he's got dark brown hair, with a mustache and goatee."

"They're funneling the counterfeit money through this casino."

"It's certainly a possibility."

She fumbled with her purse. "Well, here— Oh, God, it's not in here. The money is—"

"I have it."

"How—"

"I slipped it into my pocket while we were talking."

"You think you're pretty damn clever, don't you?"

"Mmm. Sometimes." He flipped his cigarette into the river, then straightened, wrapping both arms around her waist. "We're supposed to be making out," he said, sliding his lips along her jaw.

She glared at him, but said nothing.

He lowered his head and covered her mouth with his. Tasting her was akin to shooting adrenaline directly into his veins. He didn't even want to consider there would come a time when he couldn't touch her this way. He slid his tongue against hers and pulled her tighter against his chest. Her breathing quickened, and she returned his caress, sweet moans coming from the back of her throat.

When he pulled back for a gulp of air, his body had hardened and his blood was roaring.

"It's like kissing a damn ashtray," she muttered.

Surprisingly amused rather than irritated, he leaned his forehead against hers. "Oh, baby, that's so romantic."

She grabbed his hand and whispered, "Let's go inspect some money."

They walked along the deck a few feet, then nearly ran into someone coming from the other direction. The cowboy from the poker game.

Gage had to look up to meet his dark gaze, shadowed by the black Stetson. He'd seemed large at the table, but on his feet Gage judged him to be about six-five and two hundred–plus pounds. Muscles bulged from his forearms, exposed by the rolled-up sleeves of his tan, Western-style shirt.

"You play a hell of a poker game, slick," he said, inclining his head.

His senses already on heightened alert, Gage tightened his hold on Roxanne's hand. "Thanks."

Smiling, the cowboy stuck out his hand, which

Gage shook without releasing Roxanne. "I'm Steele Rogers. Well, actually, my real name's Nathan, but nobody calls me that if they wanna continue to walk upright. Aren't you Gage?" Before Gage could do more than freeze, the cowboy continued, "We have a mutual friend—Campbell Devereaux."

"Oh, yeah, good ol' Campbell." Even as relief coursed through him, he cursed his father. He'd said he would send an agent to watch Roxanne while Gage searched Stephano's "florist" and said only that Gage would know him. He'd never seen Steele here in his life, but he was no doubt his father's man. Campbell was his father's middle name and Devereaux was his mother's maiden name. "How about I buy you a drink?"

"I could use a whiskey."

As the trio walked toward the bar, Gage took a brief moment to admire Agent Rogers's easy demeanor and efficient approach. He could fault his father for plenty, but training top-notch undercover agents wasn't one of them.

Roxanne squeezed his arm, and he glanced at her, noting the worried look in her eyes. "You want some more champagne, baby?"

She smiled weakly. "Sure."

He kissed her cheek. "It's fine," he said low. "Steele's a close buddy of my dad's."

Her gaze cut to his, understanding dawned, and she mutely nodded.

Once they were seated at the semicircle bar, Gage made the introductions between Marina and Steele. He had no doubt his father had briefed the agent extensively on Roxanne, their relationship and the mess of this weekend, but he wanted her to understand Steele could be trusted—with her life, if necessary.

Especially since he was about to leave her with him.

ROXANNE STUDIED the profile of Nathan "Steele" Rogers—Agent Rogers, she assumed—and wondered where, exactly, he hid his gun.

This information was critical, since, as soon as she found an appropriate weapon, she was going to shoot one of his fellow agents. Several times, if she could get away with it.

She sipped her champagne, fuming over how thoroughly she'd been duped. Gage knew her too well. He'd abandoned her in public, making sure the bartender and the other customers around them heard his extra-loud announcement that he had to run to the office to pick up a fax and would his "good buddy" Steele watch over his "lady." She might be furious enough to storm out of the casino, jeopardizing Gage's case, but she'd never sacrifice Agent Rogers as well. He thought she was so smart.

Of course, Gage likely didn't know his exit had also been observed by someone else they knew—Toni. That interfering little blonde had darted after him like a slippery cat. What if one of Stephano's men had also seen her? What if she confronted Gage? The possibilities had her heart racing in anger and fear.

Through a rushed and whispered conversation with Steele, she'd tried to convince him of the danger. She had to get to her friend. She had to warn Gage. The stubborn giant had simply smiled and assured her everything would be all right and wouldn't the little lady like another glass of champagne?

Of all the nerve. Well, she fully intended to get out of this casino, with or without the cowboy next to her, find her best friend before she got them all killed, then find her ex-fiancé, who was no doubt skulking about Stephano's warehouse, and give them both a piece of her mind.

"That's a lovely necklace, Marina," Steele said cheerfully.

Her hand automatically reached for the pendant. "Thanks." She didn't want to think about the guilt connected with the jewelry or remember the hurt and anger in Gage's eyes when she'd rejected his gift. She was having a hard enough time justifying sneaking away and making Agent Rogers look bad in the process. Maybe Gage had noticed Toni and sent her on her way.

Maybe, but she couldn't take that chance.

She glanced toward the exit, calculating its distance and her chances against Steele's long legs and her speed in four-inch heels.

"Don't try it," he said low, his gaze fixed on hers.

She clenched her hand around the stem of her glass. "What?"

"Makin' a break for it."

Damn, damn, damn. So the muscle-bound cowboy wasn't near as easygoing as he seemed. Flipping her hair over her shoulder, she said, "I have no idea what you're talking about."

Steele sipped his whiskey, glancing casually around. "Gage knows what he's doin'. You don't have to worry about him."

"I'm not worried." Well, she was, but mostly she knew she was missing all the action. She wanted to be there when he uncovered the counterfeiting equipment, when he found boxes of paper and supplies...when Toni surprised him, and one of Stephano's goons caught him snooping around and—

She squeezed Steele's forearm—well, as much as one could squeeze steel—and whispered urgently, "Can't we at least call him? Warn him?"

He shook his head. "He won't have his phone on."

A ringing phone, even a vibrating phone, could interrupt warehouse snooping, she guessed. "Come with me," she begged. "I know where he is. He needs help. My friend—"

"No." He tipped his hat back, so she could finally see his eyes. They were a very vivid light blue and somehow communicated hardness and sympathy at the same time. She also noted a lock of wavy, jet-black hair had fallen over his forehead. Steele was one hunk of man. "He'll notice her. He's very good at his job," he went on. "Practically a legend in the service."

An odd sense of pride moved through her. "A legend, really?"

He patted her hand. "Really. We have orders that must be followed."

"And you always follow orders?"

He didn't even blink. "Yes, ma'am."

She sincerely doubted that, but her mind was still too busy spinning an escape to worry about questioning.

In between small sips of whiskey, Steele launched into a monologue about poker and the wild fun of Bourbon Street, which she only half listened to, but figured the topic was more for the benefit of the patrons around them instead of her anyway.

Clearly, running wasn't an option. The vision of her tripping across the casino in her heels, then being jerked off her feet in one fell swoop by the long arm of Agent Steele wasn't her idea of wise. She'd have to be more subtle and clever.

She was jolted from her thoughts when a woman fell against her, spilling her cup of nickels on the floor. Steele steadied her, and Roxanne helped her retrieve her nickels.

"Th-thank you," she said as she took the cup, leaning heavily on Steele and giving him a glassy smile.

Good grief, that woman didn't need more time at the slots. She needed a nice long nap and some Extra Strength Tylenol.

The moment the thought was out, Roxanne cut her gaze to her own glass of champagne. *Ah-ha.*

While Steele continued his efforts to keep the woman on her feet, Roxanne jumped back on her stool, picked up her glass, pretended to drink, then poured the contents into the ficus tree next to her.

The bartender had set a full glass in front of her as Steele returned to his seat.

"So," she said brightly, "you're a good poker player?"

His eyes narrowed suspiciously, but he launched into a story about some casino in Vegas where he'd won ten thousand dollars on one hand. Roxanne only half listened. Mostly, she drank champagne, turning away from Steele every so often on the pretense of looking around the room to pour some into the plant.

After draining two glasses in ten minutes and in the process of asking for a third, Steele commented, "You ought to slow down."

She gulped down nearly half the glass. "No thanks." Then her head promptly spun. She gripped the bar. At this rate, she really was going to be sick. "You ever been to Atlantic City?"

Off to another story, Roxanne had to wonder if the man really was a world champion gambler, or if he was making up all this stuff on the spot.

When ten more minutes had passed, she clutched her stomach. "I think I'm going to be sick."

Steele just sighed. "Told ya."

"I need to go to the ladies' room."

Steele rose, assisting her off her stool. "Come on."

She'd figured she wouldn't be lucky enough to go alone, so she could only pray there was a back way out of the bathroom.

"Do you want me to call someone for help?" he asked as they stopped outside the ladies'-room door.

"No." She gripped the doorknob and tried to smile. "I'll be fine."

Crossing his arms over his massive chest, he leaned against the wall. "I'll be here."

Naturally. She wobbled a bit for effect as she walked through the doorway, though she didn't have to fake the shaking of her hands. In truth, her stomach jumped around as if a family of frogs had decided to take up residence. She was about to evade a Federal Officer. What would her father say?

Nothing. Since she never intended for him to find out.

The second the door was closed behind her, she picked up the pace, finding two women applying lipstick at the mirror in the lounge area. Scooting around them, she rushed into the room with the stalls—three on one side, two on the other.

And, on the back wall, a small window.

She clenched her fists. *"Yes."*

The window was about four feet off the ground, and it was small, so she'd have to get up there and wriggle through the opening, but she'd manage.

She darted toward the back wall, flicking the locks open, then she gripped the ledge and hoisted herself up. Through the glass, she saw the sparkling night sky and the riverboat railing. *Oh, yes.*

Heart pounding, she braced herself on the ledge with her forearms and lifted the window. A brisk, cooling breeze rushed in from outside. Freedom, Toni and Gage were within her reach. She dropped back to the floor of the bathroom to remove her shoes, thanking God she'd worn pants and wouldn't be exposing all her parts to anyone who happened to walk by the window in the next couple of minutes. Including Steele.

Urged on by that thought, she gripped her shoes in one hand and levered herself back up. With a bit of straining, she managed to rest the edge of her butt on the windowsill, then swing her legs through the opening.

Her feet dangled above the deck. Her pulse pounded. She was almost there.

"Anyone in here named Marina?" a lady called from the other room.

Well, hell.

Before she'd barely had time to swear, the same lady gasped, "Oh, my."

Roxanne turned to see an elderly lady in a pale blue

pantsuit, clutching a large straw bag and staring in her direction. "Hot in here, huh?" she said lamely.

"I, uh— Yes." Looking a bit wary, she walked a few steps closer. "Are you Marina?"

Roxanne thought about lying, or saying nothing at all and just wiggling through the window. But Steele had undoubtedly sent the lady to check on her, and if she reported her escape through the window, he'd be after her in a blink. *Damn.* She had to get to Gage and Toni. She could be confronting him at this very moment, blowing his cover, risking way more than she knew about.

She glanced back at the lady. Her blue eyes were dark with concern. Then again maybe this could work to her advantage and buy her some time.

Roxanne bit her lip, trying to look frightened. "Steele sent you, didn't he?"

"A large gentleman in a cowboy hat asked me to come in and check on you. He seemed to think you were sick." Her look communicated how skeptical she'd become with this scenario.

Roxanne cast her gaze downward. "He's my boyfriend, but he...he hits me."

The lady gasped, laying her small, veiny hand on Roxanne's arm. "Oh, dear. Is there anything I can do? Should we call the police? I can't believe... He seemed so nice and concerned."

"He's like that sometimes. But then he'll start drinking again and...and..." She pretended to choke up with emotion.

"Tell me no more, dear." The lady fumbled through her bag. "I have a Glock 9 mm in here somewhere—"

"No, no. Oh, please, no." Roxanne waved her hand.

"I just need a few minutes to get away. I already moved my stuff out of the apartment. I'm moving back home with my mother."

The lady smiled. "You sweet girl. I have three of my own, grown now, of course, with four lovely grandchildren. I have pictures."

Roxanne gripped the edge of the sill, readying herself for the drop to the ground. "Maybe some other time. Just tell him I'm getting sick, but I think I'll be fine. Ask him to get me some ice water."

"Are you sure I can't do anything else?" She reached into her bag again. "I have some money."

"No, thank you." She really hated deceiving this sweet woman, but she had to get to Gage. He needed her. He was in danger. And he was dead meat for deserting her. "Just stall."

Then, before the lady could say anything more, Roxanne arched her back and slithered through the open window. Barefoot, she dropped to the deck of the boat. She was near the back, and the area was deserted. After closing the window, she padded to the corner, peeked around as she slid on her shoes, then casually, but quickly, strode toward the gangplank. Even as her knees shook and her heart pounded, she forced herself to keep her face forward and not draw undue attention to herself.

She kept waiting to hear Steele's deep voice, feel his large hand on her arm, and she worried about him getting into trouble for losing her. But no one said anything to her. No one tried to stop her.

A thrill unlike anything she'd ever felt before soared through her veins. She'd done it. She'd *actually* done it. Roxanne Lewis, CPA, a nice quiet girl from

Metairie had just outfoxed a Secret Service agent and was on her way to tracking down another so she could help him bust up a mob counterfeit ring.

As the gangplank met the sidewalk, she smiled, then held up her hand to signal a cab.

10

ROXANNE PAID the driver and alighted from the cab at the corner of Royal and St. Peter.

Her nerves were back and her confidence waning. There was no sign of Toni. Had she really managed to follow Gage? Where *was* that woman?

At least the street wasn't deserted. Many of the art galleries would no doubt be closed this time of night. But a busy restaurant sat on the corner, and there were people walking down the block and window-shopping. The Quarter was notorious for having a posh restaurant in one spot, then, a mere half a block later, could sit a sleazy strip joint, or worse, a row of vacant shops. Drug dealers and pickpockets hung out in deserted areas, even as a wild party could be going on a few feet away.

She started at the restaurant, describing Toni to the hostess. No luck there. She looked around for a bit, but saw no sign of her. Dear heaven, had she really followed Gage into the florist? There was only one way to find out.

Outside, she fought against her fears. She rolled her shoulders back and slipped through the crowd outside the restaurant, stumbling a bit as she tried to gain her footing on the uneven sidewalk. These shoes were going to make prowling difficult.

Be bold, Marina.

If anyone questioned her, she was just a lost tourist. Simple. Direct. Innocent.

She fell into step behind a young couple and peered into the same gallery window they did, then cast her glance sideways to count the number of shops between her and the florist. Three. Only three more doors.

Looking around with a casual air, she clutched her purse to her side and continued down the block, making sure she stayed behind the couple. When she reached the gallery window next to the florist, she pretended fascination with an oil painting of a jazz musician playing a sax.

She glanced to the side, noting the darkened window of the florist. Her heart hammered. She took two steps in that direction. She was really going to give Toni a piece of her—

A hand closed over her mouth. Someone yanked her into the dark alley between the two buildings.

She drew a breath to scream, realized how ineffective that would be and instinctively jabbed her elbow back instead. And encountered a hard wall of a stomach.

"You should probably be aiming lower, babe," a familiar voice said in her ear.

She went limp in Gage's arms. "You scared me to death!"

He dragged her away from the street. When they reached a small, dimly lit courtyard at the back of the building, he spun her around to face him. He smiled, but not reassuringly. "Just what the hell do you think you're doing here?"

She pressed her hand against her chest, trying to

calm her racing heart. "Helping you. God, did you have to grab me like that?" She glanced up at him. His steady gaze was focused on her face. He wasn't even breathing hard. "You don't seem very surprised to see me."

"I've known you were coming for twenty minutes."

Huh? Toni hadn't known she was coming either. Still... "Toni?"

"Bumbled along behind me for about four steps before I saw her. I put her in a cab. Steele's going to her house to make sure she gets home."

Whew. One thing off her conscience, and obviously she hadn't caused Gage any real trouble. Still, how had he known she'd show up? "Steele called you," she decided.

"He did. But I expect I knew even before he did."

She creased her forehead, knowing she must be missing something but at a loss to figure out where she'd gone wrong.

Gage lifted her diamond and emerald pendant, rubbing his thumb over the jewels. "At least I know I was right not to tell you, or this lovely piece would have no doubt wound up at the bottom of the Mississippi."

"Will you stop talking in riddles and just tell me what the devil you're talking about?"

He tapped the pendant with his finger, then released it and her. "Your necklace, my dear, is a tracking device."

Her mouth fell open. "You bugged me?" She held up the jeweled pendant, narrowing her eyes in an attempt to spot something out of place.

"I worried you might try exactly what you did, and though I gave little chance of you succeeding, it seems my instincts for backup were justified. Wish I'd thought to do the same to Toni. By the way, you're lucky I grabbed you before the muggers who hang out on this street did."

"You *bugged* me?" she repeated, her temper spiking as her pride sank. She thought she'd been so clever to get away from Steele, and yet Gage knew where she was the whole time. She'd wanted to help him, show him she could handle herself.

"You're also lucky I got you before Steele did. He's not pleased with your little scam. He told me to tell you that lady you spoke to in the bathroom smacked him with her big straw bag, and he barely escaped the casino before she called the police."

With her own pride bruised handily, she could understand Steele's frustration. "It's your fault, you know." She pointed her finger at him. "If you hadn't abandoned me, I wouldn't have had to take such drastic measures."

He slid his hands in his pants pockets and sighed. "This is no place for you, Rox."

"I still want to know why you bugged me, why you thought it necessary to violate my civil rights." Fury roared through her body. She stood toe-to-toe with him. "I'm not a dog to be tracked. You don't have any hold on me, or any right to know what I do or who I do it with. I want to know why, Gage. *Why?*"

"So I'd never lose you," he said quietly.

Well, hell. She dropped her head forward, resting her cheek on his chest. Tears pricked the back of her eyes. Why couldn't life be simple? Why couldn't she just wrap her arms around him, hold him until the world just fell away, until nothing mattered but touching him, keeping him close to her heart? "The fact that I now think this is the most romantic thing you've ever done should tell you how out of sorts I am."

He wrapped his arms tight around her and kissed the top of her head. "I love you, Rox, and you scared me to death. What were you thinking about, coming here and—"

"You *what?*" She grabbed the front of his shirt. "What did you just say?"

"I—" Confusion slid into his eyes. Then he went still, obviously realizing the words he'd let escape. He cupped her face in his palms, his gaze penetrating hers with an emotion she'd only let herself wonder and dream about. There was honesty and raw emotion behind those dark eyes, and her heart pounded with the implications. "I love you, Roxanne. I want to spend my life with you. Always. Forever."

"You do?" she said inanely.

"I know I don't say the words often."

"No, Gage, you never say them. *Never.*" Her voice grew in strength as she recalled the insecurities that had always plagued her. "When I tell you I love you after making love, you just kiss my forehead. Like you're placating me. Like you understand my devotion but can't return it in kind. I'm never really sure how you feel. You mumbled about love. You avoided it."

He looked up and around. "Why are we having this conversation in a courtyard behind a mob-owned florist?"

She gripped his jaw, bringing his face back toward hers. "Oh, no, you don't. Tell me. Tell me, dammit!

What do I really mean to you other than an intelligent dinner companion, a decent cook and a good lay?''

He pushed her away and bit out a few choice cusswords—in Italian, she thought. He speared his hand through his hair. He muttered to the dark, star-filled sky about his case, the timing, the bad guys who might be looming. Finally, he faced her. His eyes, though brown instead of the silver of the real man, were fierce with determination. ''Yes, I love you. More than's probably wise for a man like me. Most of the time I don't understand it.'' He took a deep breath, then pushed on. ''When my mother left us, my father said we didn't need her. We could make our own life. I wrote her letters. I begged her to come back. I told her how much I loved her and wanted her part of my life.'' His breath shuddered out. ''She never answered.''

Roxanne's knees buckled, but she kept herself upright because she didn't want him to know how much she pitied the boy he'd been. She'd given her heart to a man who'd lied, kept secrets and had a dark side, but he also had vulnerabilities. The fact that he was finally sharing them with her brought harsh tears to her eyes.

''I swore I'd never give that much of myself to anyone again,'' he practically shouted at her. ''Then you came along. And, hell, I just...I forgot all those vows.'' He shoved his hands in his pockets. His gaze held her transfixed. ''I more than love you. I *need* you. Without you, I can't seem to make anything else matter.''

''Gage, I—'' She took two, halting steps toward him, then threw her arms around his neck. The feel of his strong, hard body next to hers, of his arms holding her as if he'd never let her go, reassured her of the future. Could they really work through their differences? Could she find a place in his world and him in hers? "I love you. I need you. I just—"

He laid his finger against her lips. "Stop."

She kissed his jaw. "I know we still have a lot to work out. I don't know how this whole cop thing is going to work. I can't imagine living with—"

"Shut up, Rox."

She glared at him. "Hey, you got to pour your heart out. I need my turn."

He reached into his pants pocket. "My phone's vibrating."

"Well, damn, I told Steele—" She stopped, realizing explaining her idea of contacting him via phone was a moot point now.

"Yeah," Gage said into the phone. Then he swore. "How the hell did that happen?" He paced away from her. "Hey, man, you're the one who has to explain that to the Secretary." He flipped the phone closed, returning it to his pocket.

There was no way that could have been good. "What?"

"Stephano ditched our tail. The other agents figure we've got an hour."

"An hour for what?"

"To search that florist and confirm the evidence we need is inside." He grabbed her hand. "Come on."

Before she'd done more than process the turn in events, he'd stalked down the alley. Then, outside the florist, with her body hiding his actions, he disarmed the security system, and they slipped inside.

She stood silently as he prowled around for a few

minutes, checking the back door and access to the courtyard, then opening a door on the right side of the shop. It was a small storeroom. Metal shelving containing boxes and paper lined one wall, a mop and bucket rested in the corner, more boxes in the other, ribbons and bows were scattered across a bulletin board on the back wall.

As he laid his hand on top of one of the boxes, they heard the sound of approaching voices.

Gage went dead still. Roxanne's heart hammered. The voices grew louder.

She glanced out of the room in time to see two shadows moving in front of the shop.

Gage pointed to the corner. "Behind those boxes." He flipped off the overhead light and shut the door.

A second later, he crouched next to her, and she tuned her ears to any sound besides the rapid beat of her heart. She'd come to help him and Toni, but she'd only disrupted the investigation, slowed things down, distracted him.

Was that a scrape? A key turning in a lock?

Then a voice said, "That girl at the club wanted you, man."

Roxanne sucked in a breath. Good grief. She'd been asking Gage for heartfelt confessions, and their lives were in imminent danger. Why hadn't she just stayed at the casino with Steele?

Gage kissed her temple. "It's okay."

Roxanne held her breath and fought to keep her emotions under control.

"By the way," Gage whispered in her ear, his warm breath at least confirming they were alive for the moment. "You're a *great* lay."

Roxanne sunk lower behind the rows of boxes as she heard the two men talking in the outer room. *Super. My dad can inscribe that on my tombstone.*

GAGE REACHED alongside his calf for his gun. It wasn't much. A small revolver, but risking his government-issue 9 mm wasn't an option with the concealment he needed.

On impulse, he also drew out his backup revolver from his other calf holster and handed the gun to Roxanne. "Just in case," he whispered.

Wrinkling her nose, she held the butt between her thumb and index finger. "In case what? I don't know anything about guns."

Gage huffed out a breath and peered over the boxes, his gaze locked on the door. "How do you grow up in a houseful of cops and not know how to fire a gun?"

"On purpose."

"Aim midbody and keep pulling the trigger until somebody falls down."

This is where love gets you—trapped in a storeroom with six bullets and an accountant for backup.

He tuned his ears to the sounds coming from the shop. He only heard muttering and something sliding across the floor. A box or crate maybe? How long did these guys plan to hang around? Before Roxanne showed up, he'd only had time to check the cabinets and coolers in the main part of the shop. He'd just started on a locked door behind the counter when his tracking device had signaled her impending arrival. He had work to do. He didn't want his attention divided between Roxanne and his job. Yet, he should have known she wouldn't stay put.

Maybe you should have taken the time to explain why you needed to investigate alone. Talk to her instead of ordering her around.

He'd be lousy at marriage. Why had he ever thought he could really have her? He'd been alone a long time and wasn't sure he could change, be the kind of man she needed.

Yet, despite everything they'd been through in the last two days, despite his lies and mistakes, she loved him. Still. The cynical side of him—well, actually, in his case a "side" was more like three-fourths—didn't believe that would be enough. But an odd kind of hope and wonder also moved through his veins. A feeling he couldn't shove aside or deny.

The doorknob rattled. "We need that other box?" a voice asked.

"Yeah."

Gage ducked completely behind the boxes. His muscles tensed. He slid his finger to the trigger.

He could hear Roxanne's shallow breathing behind him. *Hang on, baby.*

The door creaked. "Hey, Theodore, think I ought to get two?"

"Whatever" came the gruff answer from the outer room.

Ridiculously, all Gage could think was *Theodore?* What kind of name was Theodore for a mobster?

The door creaked again and shuffling footsteps entered the storeroom. Gage willed his breathing to slow. His heart pounded so loud he was certain the sound echoed around the room. He kept his hand steady on his revolver and braced himself for potential confrontation.

The shuffling stopped. The intruder was standing on the right, in front of the metal shelves, Gage thought. Something slid, then a grunt, like a man lifting a heavy box, then the shuffling footsteps faded. The footsteps returned seconds later, followed by what Gage supposed was the man lifting the second heavy item.

It was several long minutes before the man returned to the storeroom again. Beads of sweat rolled down Gage's back. The guy paused in the center of the room. Gage held his breath. Then the light cord was pulled, plunging the room again into darkness as the measured footsteps faded toward the door. The lock in the doorknob clicked; the door closed.

Gage reached back and grabbed Roxanne's hand, finding her skin cold. "Wait," he whispered.

She squeezed his hand in return, and he allowed himself a small sigh of relief. They'd gotten lucky. But he also knew they were far from safe. Panic tried to bust through his tension, but from long experience he stifled the weakness. His tenacity was vital to their survival.

As the pulse in Roxanne's wrist beat in time with his, he realized he could also draw strength from her. He hadn't relied on anyone in a long, long time. It was a wonder, and a relief, that he knew he could do so now. He could trust her. And really, wasn't that what love and marriage was all about?

"Boss want 'em in back?"

Gage shook aside his distracted musings and tuned in to the voice of the guy who'd come into the storeroom.

"Yeah," returned Theodore. "The Boy Wonder needs 'em for tomorrow."

The Boy Wonder? Mettles? Or maybe nephew Stephano.

Someone unlocked another door—the one behind the counter, or the one down the hall leading to the alley, since the sound came from the right, and the front door was on Gage's left.

"What's going on?" Roxanne whispered next to his ear.

Despite their dire situation, Gage's sensual nerve endings stood at attention. The warmth of her breath, the closeness of her body devoured his concentration, and all the more enticing because of the complete darkness of their surroundings.

"They're moving something into the back," he said. "Or maybe into a car in the alley."

"But what—"

"Shh."

Several minutes passed in silence. Then more shuffling steps. Another door opened, then closed seconds later.

Gage rolled his shoulders back. His ankles felt tingly, on the verge of going to sleep, so he shifted his stance. Roxanne squeezed his hand, then let go, as if sensing his need for freedom of movement.

"Don't know why there's so much rush all of a sudden." This comment was from Theodore.

"Boss does seem anxious," the other guy commented.

Yeah. Now that he's got my—strike that, the government's—*hundred-thousand-dollar wire transfer.*

So, the big question remained, just what was being

rushed? Stephano had his hand in any number of legal and illegal operations. But this had to be connected to the counterfeiting, especially in light of the actions he'd witnessed at the casino and the evidence recovered at the electronics store. But he needed more than a handful of funny money. He needed a connection to Stephano. This property was it.

He worried, though. Even if he found something incriminating, would it be enough? Stephano had circumvented the law many times. He'd escaped federal prosecution one way or another—a witness suddenly missing or dead, a payoff, evidence missing—so many times, the Feds had screamed for results. Which, of course, had brought about his undercover investigation in the first place.

He'd be a hero if he brought Stephano in. But suddenly all he wanted was to get him and Roxanne out alive.

A door slammed, then the two men walked across the shop. The front door opened, then closed. The lock clicked into place.

But Gage refused to relax. He waited, listening to the silence, the occasional muffled laughter or conversation from someone passing by the shop outside. Roxanne stroked the inside of his wrist with her thumb. He wasn't sure she was really aware of the comforting motion, but he absorbed her touch nevertheless.

When the silence extended for over three minutes, which he timed by his watch, he turned to Roxanne and pushed a button on his watch that flicked on a small stream of light.

Her chin, the line of her jaw, illuminated. He

couldn't see her eyes and doubted she could see his. "I still need to look around, and I don't have much time. Wanna stay here?"

"I don't *think* so." She crumpled the front of his shirt in her fist. "Try to lose me again and lose a vital part of your anatomy."

He smiled. "You know, this weekend has brought out a deep-seated aggression in you that I don't think either of us was aware of before."

She adjusted her grip, clenching the fabric tighter against his throat. "Having your life and future threatened will do that to a woman."

"But examining your reaction, you must admit a certain...liberation on your part."

She angled her head. "Maybe. I'll admit this weekend seems to have brought out my wilder side."

He thought back to the moments in the lingerie-shop dressing room, their lovemaking in the hotel. Again, he smiled. "A bit." He leaned toward her, brushing his lips against her cheek. "You're incredible."

"I could get used to you saying that."

"Please do." He kissed her lips lightly, then reluctantly pulled away. "I need to get to work."

"I'll help." She rose, then extended her hand to him. "Why were those guys here? I thought we had an hour."

"The agent who called was following Stephano. I thought we had all his cronies covered, but obviously not."

"Well, let's just hope they stay gone."

He stood, and holding her hand, pulled the cord to

the light. "Let's see what those guys were so anxious to move."

He approached the shelves, noting that the third one from the bottom, which had been full of boxes, now seemed to have a couple missing. Gage lifted one of the remaining three, finding it solid and fairly heavy—twenty-five to thirty pounds—and set it on the floor. His heart raced as he lifted the lid.

"Paper?" Roxanne said in confusion when the contents were exposed.

Gage's heart rate kicked up even higher. Careful to handle only the edges so he wouldn't smear any fingerprints, he picked up the top sheet of paper. He rubbed his thumb across one corner, noting the distinctive feel and the red and blue fibers scattered across the surface. He'd bet his badge the paper in his hand weighed exactly one gram—the same weight as each and every United States bill.

"A very special kind of paper," he said. "One I'll bet the BEP wouldn't be pleased to see outside of Washington."

"The BEP?"

"The Bureau of Engraving and Printing."

Roxanne gasped. "This is a box of unprinted money."

"Looks like."

Excited now, she patted his arm. "It's illegal to have this paper here."

"Oh, yeah."

"This is the evidence you need. You can arrest Stephano."

He hated to douse her enthusiasm. "I could have arrested him dozens of times over the last six months.

This is a great break. We can link this property to him, and this property possesses illegal products, but we need more. I want the printer, the distinctive green ink—which, incidentally, is supposed to be almost impossible to duplicate without the original formula—and the computer that designed it all.''

"You think all that stuff is here somewhere?"

"There's only one way to find out." He returned the paper to the box, then set the box back on the shelf.

"You're not taking the paper?"

"I'll get it with a search warrant. We need to get moving." After turning off the light and listening for a moment at the door, he turned the knob. In the main part of the shop, he again disarmed the alarm by the door with a special scrambler, then headed for the door behind the counter, tucking his gun behind his belt and pulling a set of picks from his pocket.

"You can pick a lock?"

He glanced back at Roxanne. "It comes in handy sometimes."

In seconds, he had the door opened. As he walked around the room, he used the light on his watch to scope out the inside, which appeared to be a small, cluttered office. A desktop computer, an ordinary ink-jet printer, filing cabinets, invoices stacked on the desk, a rolling office chair, a small refrigerator in the corner. No boxes like the ones in the storeroom.

"Flip on the light, would you?" he asked Roxanne. *Damn.* He was sure those guys had brought the boxes in here. The only other place they could have gone was out the back door, but why would they have taken them out there when they'd arrived and left by the front door?

"It's an office," Roxanne said matter-of-factly. She narrowed her eyes as she glanced around. "And where are the boxes?"

Frustrated, Gage shrugged. "Hell if I know."

She clapped her hands. "Hey, maybe there's a secret room." She immediately crossed to the wall and ran her hands over the wood paneling.

"Rox, this isn't a Nancy Drew novel."

She ignored him and kept tapping her hands across the wall, working her way around the room.

Gage picked the locks on each file cabinet, then thumbed through the files. And found zilch. He tunneled his hand through his hair. This couldn't be everything. He was close to the heart of this operation. He could almost taste it.

Roxanne stopped tapping suddenly. "Good grief, I almost forgot. What did you do with that money from the casino?"

"It's still in my pocket. Why?"

"Well? Is it counterfeit?"

"It's fake."

"More evidence. Surely with that, plus the paper…"

Gage shook his head. "The money just gave me cause for a search warrant of the casino." He shoved his hands into his pockets. "Which I thought I could order for tomorrow, maybe even later tonight. But we've got to connect this place to the casino first."

Roxanne crossed her arms over her chest and leaned back against the wall. "This detective business is frustrating."

Those were the last words she said before the wall gave way and Roxanne disappeared through it.

11

ROXANNE BLINKED, noting she was lying on her back in a narrow, dimly lit hallway.

Gage appeared next to her. His eyes were dark with concern. "Rox, talk to me. Are you all right? Can you move?"

"I think so." She lifted her arms and bent her legs, then rolled her head from side the side. "What happened?"

Gage helped her to a sitting position. "Apparently we *are* in the middle of a Nancy Drew novel."

She glanced over to the section of wall she'd fallen through, which was actually a hinged door, then around the hall. At the far end sat, amazingly, a spiral staircase that wound toward a twenty-foot-high ceiling and ended at a metal platform and door. "A secret staircase?"

"I think that's *The Crooked Banister*."

"What do you know about Nancy Drew mysteries?"

Gage helped her to her feet. "I always went for the smart women, even in elementary school."

Roxanne smiled. "Is that a compliment?"

He stroked her cheek. "Absolutely."

Turning away from the tender look on his face, which she wasn't sure how to deal with at the moment, she dusted off her pants, noting a snag in the delicate lace. The outfit wasn't exactly practical for warehouse skulking. "So, you think we've hit the jackpot?" she asked as he closed the concealed door.

He slid his hand against her back, urging her toward the staircase. "I don't think there's a big collection of mums up there."

With one foot on the bottom stair, she glanced up, and her stomach jolted. "Who do you think is up there?"

"Probably nobody," he said, though he pulled his gun from his belt. Then he looked at her, his eyes dead serious. "You can go back to the hotel if you want."

She hitched her purse on her shoulder, feeling comfort for the first time in her life that a deadly weapon lay inside her bag, and swallowed the fear fighting to emerge. "I'm sticking."

Gage led the way up the metal winding stairs. Roxanne followed on tiptoe so her heels wouldn't get caught in the grates, and held tight to the railing for balance. At the door, her heart raced not only from the climb, but the anticipation and panic of what lay just beyond the door.

Gage briefly rested his ear against the door frame, examined the frame, then knelt and went to work on the lock with his picks. She held her breath.

Seconds later, he stood. "If an alarm goes off, you run like hell."

She simply nodded.

He turned the knob slowly, pushing the door open a crack. No alarm. No sounds from the other side of the door. Gun in one hand, he grabbed hers with the other and slipped inside.

They found themselves standing on a high metal

landing, which let to a catwalk that encircled the room. Stairs to the right let to the floor. Lights overhead illuminated the concrete wall and floor-lined warehouse where a maze of boxes and crates, many of them shaped like paintings, covered the ground. Some paintings and sculptures had been removed from their containers and lay against the walls.

Obviously they were in the back of the gallery next door to the florist.

Though thankfully no bad guys rushed into view, she also didn't see any sign of the equipment they were after, or the boxes of paper the two goons had carried from the florist's storeroom. The only sound she heard was the quiet, consistent hum of the lights. "Where—"

Gage held his finger to his lips and gestured down the stairs with the barrel of his gun.

She followed his directions, using the same care she had on the other staircase. When they reached the floor, he again held her hand as they moved cautiously along the rows of containers. They stayed low and Gage constantly glanced up toward the door they'd entered. At least if someone barged in, they had plenty of hiding spots.

Then they rounded the corner of a row of crates on the right side of the warehouse and hit the real jackpot.

Half a dozen folding tables were lined in a row, computer equipment covering the surfaces. Cords and wires snaked and looped across monitors with several types and sizes of screens. Large computer towers and printers were all hooked together. The two boxes like the ones in the storeroom sat underneath the first table. Stacks of uncut, printed twenty-dollar bills covered the last.

Gage had been right. No giant printing press. No plates. This whole operation was being run by no more computer equipment than she'd seen at most insurance companies.

Even as he started toward the tables, Gage was punching numbers on his cell phone. "I need that search warrant now, sir," he said briefly. He listened for a moment, then described what he'd found.

Watching him work, Roxanne hung back. His energy permeated the room. He moved with controlled efficiency and grace. He was dark and sexy and interesting.

How could she let him go?

This weekend had enlightened her with so much about him. Living with cops her whole life, she understood his drive, dedication and focus. She couldn't ask him to change. But she didn't think she could change herself either. Now that she understood the dangers so intimately, she'd fear for him even more. They could never have a normal life together. His cases could start and end at any time.

Daddy will be back in four months, honey. He has to go infiltrate an Internet scam in Wyoming.

Or what if the Treasury Department decided to transfer him to the presidential detail? He could spend his days walking around in a blue suit and sunglasses with an Uzi under his jacket.

She shuddered.

Though her heart was breaking into pieces, she knew she had to stay strong. She had to find again the peace she'd held on to for so long.

He loves you, and you're going to let him down. Like his father, you'll ignore his feelings. Like his mother, you'll desert him.

At the end of one row of containers, she sank to the floor, leaning her back against a crate. Dammit, what other choice did she have?

Those knee-weakening thoughts probably saved her life.

"Well, well, Mr. Angelini," said a smooth, familiar voice. "Or should I say Detective Angelini?"

Peeking around the corner of the crate, Roxanne gasped when Stephano strolled into view, a nasty-looking black pistol clutched in his hand.

As Gage flipped his cell phone closed, she jerked her head back, staring straight ahead at the wall, her heart racing, her mind spinning horrible scenarios, even as she fought to keep still and silent. She had no idea if Gage was aware of her concealed position, but she couldn't take the chance that he might instinctively glance her way. Heaven help them, she might be their only chance of survival.

Holding her breath, she slowly inched backward, working her way around the back corner of the crate.

She stopped moving and peered through a crack between two crates when she heard Stephano's voice again. "I knew there was something about you I shouldn't trust." He laughed. "And here I thought you'd come to steal my idea. A search warrant," he added, shaking his head. "Should I now assume those cops I just ditched belong to you?"

"I have backup coming," Gage said, his hand—and his gun—dangling by his side. "You might want to get lost while you can."

"Soon enough, I will," Stephano said easily. "The cops won't have an easy time getting a judge in this town to go against me and sign your warrant, giving me time to get my equipment. Oh, and kill you, of course." He smiled.

Roxanne bit her tongue to keep from screaming.

Two burly men she'd never seen before walked around a row of boxes. They took positions on opposite sides of Gage, one yanking the revolver from his hand, the other wrapping a big meaty fist around Gage's upper arm.

"We were just coming into the gallery," Stephano said. "Imagine our surprise when the alarm to the warehouse door went off."

Damn. They should have known Stephano would have the door rigged in some way, but they'd been in a rush and hadn't expected him so quickly. They'd run out of time. Gage could have done the search more quickly without her.

But you found the secret door. You helped. You just have to keep your cool now.

"I don't think the detective will be giving us any trouble, men," Stephano said. "Get Mettles and get this equipment broken down."

The goon on the right laid Gage's gun on the table, then they walked out.

"It's too bad, really," Stephano said, calmly taking aim at Gage. "I kinda liked you."

Roxanne's heart jumped into her throat. She *had* to do something *now*. She fumbled in her purse for the gun Gage had given her. Hands trembling, she aimed at Stephano from between the crates.

At that moment, Clark Mettles walked around the

row of boxes behind Gage. "Sir, I— Oh, God." He dropped to the floor, laying his hands over his head.

Roxanne let her breath out in a whoosh, but didn't lower her weapon.

Stephano sighed. "Get up, you idiot."

Mettles raised his head. "Yes, sir. Of course." He leaped to his feet. "I just didn't expect—"

"And shut up."

His shoulders slumped. "Yes, sir."

"Now get going on that—"

Gage moved lightning fast, grabbing Mettles around the neck and shielding his body with the engineer's. "Let's rethink this whole situation, gentlemen."

Behind the containers, Roxanne smiled. Gage was back in control. They would be fine. He would get them out of this.

Her positive thinking was brutally interrupted by Stephano's laughter. "Everybody's expendable, Angelini."

He pulled the trigger.

Mettles body jerked. Blood exploded from his upper chest. As he crumpled to the floor, Gage twitched, then fell to his knees.

No, no, no.

She shook her head. Tears sprang to her eyes.

Blood seemed to be everywhere—on Gage's face and neck, on his chest, down one arm. Had he been shot? Whose blood was whose?

Obviously, Stephano wasn't taking any chances. He walked forward slowly, his gun aimed to fire again.

Roxanne wasn't sure which part of her brain clicked on. A protective instinct? The inner strength her father claimed every Lewis had? Or just a plain ol' sense of furious retribution?

But she barely flinched when she fired the gun clutched in her hand.

GAGE BRACED HIMSELF for another hit as the second shot echoed through the warehouse.

But though his shoulder screamed in pain, some part of him realized Stephano's gun hadn't gone off. His eyes widened as the mobster clutched his shin and dropped to the floor.

Then Roxanne appeared from around a row of crates, her arms extended as she pointed her gun at Stephano. "Drop that gun, creep, before I shoot you again."

Obviously in agony, Stephano let go of the gun and flopped onto his back, now clutching his leg with both hands. Blood seeped through his fingers.

As Roxanne scooped up the pistol, two of Stephano's men—who must have heard the shots—raced around the boxes.

Gage dived for his own gun, scooping it off the table and squeezing off two quick shots.

The two henchmen went down like felled trees.

Now with a gun in each hand, Roxanne whirled to them. "Oh, God. Gage?"

"They're not going anywhere," he assured her, watching the blood flow from their bodies. Everything inside him revolted at the idea of her seeing such a sight. He'd exposed her to this mess, this danger.

She rushed toward him. "Are you all right?"

"Got my shoulder. I'll live." He set aside his revolver and took Stephano's pistol from her, keeping the gun trained on him. Pain pumped through his veins as surely as blood. His head swam as he knelt next to Mettles.

The front of the engineer's shirt was soaked in blood, but he had a pulse—for the moment anyway.

"It doesn't look good, does it?" Roxanne asked, her green eyes bright with worry as she crouched next to them.

"No." He worked up the strength to smile at her. "Nice shot, partner."

"It felt kind of empowering, as if that isn't weird."

"Makes perfect sense to me."

"Could we call in the cavalry now? I think I'm going to fall apart real soon."

"You'll be fine." His stomach rolled. Sweat trickled down his spine. "My cell phone. Hit redial."

She laid her hand against his cheek. "Dammit, Gage, you're turning white."

"Shock."

As her gaze jumped to his shoulder, she grabbed the phone and pressed a button. "Be still. I'll get something to make a compress with."

When she rose, Gage noted Stephano limping away. "Hold it," he commanded.

"You won't shoot me in the back," the mobster responded, still moving. "Too much paperwork."

The hell I will. For touching Roxanne alone he'd like to—

"I'm not a cop," Roxanne said. "I can shoot you in the back."

Stopping, the mob boss twisted to face her, his cold blue eyes spewing resentment. "I'll never stop hunting you down. I'll avenge this humiliation."

"Yeah, yeah, send me a postcard from Walla Walla."

Gage couldn't help a burst of pride.

She hooked the phone between her shoulder and her ear as she gathered an armful of uncut counterfeit bills, rushing back to his side. "Who is this?" she said into the receiver as she folded bills, pressing them against his shoulder.

Gage grit his teeth against the pain, even as he grabbed a stack of bills and pressed them into Mettles's chest.

"Thrilled to meet you, Colin," Roxanne continued. "I need an ambulance out here at this warehouse pronto."

"You crazy woman!" Stephano shouted, his face red and sweaty. "Those bills are worth millions."

She ignored him and directed her comment to his father. "Gage has been hit in the shoulder. He's conscious, but I need help. And I've got four other victims." She paused. "Yes, four. Two beyond hope, I think. Another with a GSW to the chest, another GSW to the leg." She paused again. "Yes, gunshot wound." Another pause, then a sigh. "No, I'm not a cop. I'm an accountant."

Sweat continued to roll down Gage's face. His mind was fuzzy. His arm had gone numb. But he fought to stay conscious as he listened to Roxanne. He had to keep Stephano at bay while she called for help, and he certainly didn't want to miss his tigress going toe-to-toe with his father, who knew exactly who she was and what she did, but his description of her as quiet and shy was probably throwing the man off, considering the bloodshed.

"Actually, he's one of the wounded." She paused, rolling her eyes. "Look, Colin, I really don't have time to explain. You could always get your in-charge butt on a plane and come down here yourself. The ambulance will take us to St. Michael's."

She pressed a button and glanced down at him. "He's a real stuffed shirt."

Gage worked up a smile. "The best."

She shook her head and dialed again. "Nine-one-one," she explained to him.

His father had no doubt connected with the local authorities and medical personnel the moment he'd gotten her call, but Gage was so impressed with Roxanne's calm, quick reasoning he didn't mention this.

"I need an ambulance and police at 86 Royal." She continued to explain to the operator about the injuries and that an officer was down. She again explained she was an accountant, not a cop, giving Gage the strength to fight back another wave of dizzying pain. "No, I won't disconnect."

But she laid the phone beside her as she knelt next to him, running her fingers through his hair. She was worried. But if she was scared, she was hiding it well. "Hang on, Gage."

"I am." He propped his good arm on his bent knee, the barrel pointing toward Stephano, who sat on the floor fifteen feet away, holding his injured leg. His eyes were still cold, but his skin had turned pasty, and a pool of blood had formed beneath his foot. "See what you can do about him."

She kissed his forehead. "I love you."

His heart jumped. He searched her eyes for something new, some sense that things had changed, that their future could be forged together. But she seemed only sad. And resigned. "Is that enough?" he asked.

"I'm not sure."

He hadn't expected any more. He shifted his gaze to Stephano and said nothing.

She sighed, picked up the phone then grabbed another stack of bills as she crossed to the mobster. She stopped a few feet from him and tossed the paper at his feet. "Use that before you pass out." She turned away just as quickly, speaking into the phone. "Still here."

Hooking the receiver between the side of her head and her shoulder, she took over applying pressure to Mettles's chest, whose pulse, Gage noted with a quick check, was growing weaker. That traitorous SOB Stephano was going to be booked on murder charges if help didn't arrive soon.

Another minute or two passed, with neither he nor Roxanne saying a word. He silently acknowledged his case was most certainly over. She'd told him earlier she wanted him to move his stuff out of the house. His big declaration of love hadn't changed a thing, it seemed. Had he really expected it to?

Yes, he had.

Sirens screamed in the distance. Dizziness washed over Gage. His hand, holding the gun, wavered. Stephano blurred before his eyes. He wanted to lie down, just for a minute, to get his strength back. But in the distance, he heard Roxanne still speaking to the 911 operator. He had to hold on, just for a few more minutes. He had to protect her.

Then suddenly he felt the cold concrete floor against his back.

Roxanne's face appeared above him. "Gage?"

Blood trickling down his arm, he reached up, working his fingers beneath the edge of her wig. Body and spirit weak, he needed to see her, the real her at that moment.

She helped him pull off the wig, then scrubbed her hands through her real hair to release the pins holding it back. The curly red strands brushed his cheek as she pressed her lips softly to his. "You're going to be fine. I won't leave you."

Not right now anyway.

But he'd lose her.

Very soon.

"DAMN YOU, Gage! Don't pass out on me now." Roxanne held his jaw, moving his head from side to side. She really wanted to panic. Tears hovered at the back of her throat and behind her eyes. His injuries were much more serious than he'd let on. He might die.

And she'd told him love might not be enough.

Her stomach pitched. She really thought she might throw up, but she knew she had to be strong for Gage.

As the sirens grew louder, she glanced at Stephano—this time trying to crawl from the room. Sick inside and her patience long gone, she simply fired a shot in his direction. The bullet slammed into a crate behind him. "Stay where you are, jerkface."

He rolled to a sitting position, slumping against the crates, probably not wanting the cops to find him on his knees in front of a woman—even one holding a gun.

"You'd better ask the cops to put you in maximum security," she said through a tear-thickened voice, "because if anything happens to him, I'm coming after you myself."

"Crazy broad," he muttered.

"Yeah. You remember that."

She heard a door slam open. "Fire department!" shouted someone from the gallery.

"Back here!" she called back, not letting go of Gage's hand.

Up until that moment, since she'd first heard Stephano's voice, time seemed to crawl. Now everything happened with amazing speed. Firefighters appeared with their axes and thick yellow coats. Paramedics rushed in with stretchers. Police with drawn guns and Kevlar vests quickly rounded up the bad guys and confiscated her gun. Only the fact that several of the people from both the fire and police departments recognized her kept her from a visit to the station for questioning.

She shook her head at their curious looks and murmurs of comfort, moving just far enough away from Gage to let the medics go to work. When they loaded him onto a stretcher, she followed them through the warehouse and gallery and out into the humid night air, where a crowd had gathered along the sidewalk. She jumped into the back of the ambulance, sinking to the floor at the foot of the stretcher while the medics continued tending Gage.

A couple of tears leaked from her eyes, but she felt calm somehow. Or maybe she was just in shock.

As they rolled down the street, she made another call on Gage's cell phone. When the commanding, serious man on the other end answered, she had to swallow before she could speak. "Daddy, I need you."

12

ROXANNE SHIFTED her backside in the orange plastic waiting-room chair. With worry lines wrinkling their foreheads, the two medics who'd brought Gage to the hospital stood in front of her. She'd gone to high school with one, and the other played poker on Thursday nights with her brother.

"You sure you don't want some coffee?" Alan, her brother's poker buddy, asked.

She linked her numb hands together in her lap. "No."

"You're...uh, that guy...is he the one you're marrying?"

Roxanne glanced at the bare finger on her left hand. She bit her lip and nodded.

He stood there next to his partner, that awkward look of bafflement on his face that every man produced when a woman was upset, and he had no control over fixing things.

She hadn't said anything about Gage to anyone other than to tell the admissions nurse his name. And even that she regretted. She had no idea what the Treasury Department wanted, but she was certain the less said, the better.

The outside world had intruded on the Hollywood soundstage her life had become. She had even less idea how to deal with Gage's secrets here.

A hand gripped her shoulder. "Roxanne?"

She glanced up into her father's worried face. She rose and turned, wrapping her arms around his waist, laying her cheek against his chest and breathing in the familiar scent of Old Spice.

"How is he?" he asked, stroking her hair.

"In surgery. The guys think he'll be okay."

Behind her, she heard the medics exchange greetings with her father. He suggested they go get something to eat, though he didn't encourage them to leave. Violence had hit close to home in their community, and they'd band together through the worst. Her father had sat in hospital emergency rooms more times than she could count, waiting on word of a fellow officer, firefighter or one of their family members.

"Yes, sir, Captain," Alan said. "Let us know if we can do anything."

When they were alone, her father asked quietly, "You want to tell me what happened?"

She looked up, meeting his gaze, his brown eyes so like hers. At least normally.

Those familiar eyes narrowed. "What are you wearing?"

She clasped his hand. "I need some air."

As they walked through the waiting room, she could feel his gaze measuring her, her Frederick's of Hollywood outfit, fake tan and heavy makeup no doubt confusing him. She wondered how much he'd been told about the shootings. He had to know who Stephano was, and word of the counterfeiting equipment was sure to have raced through the grapevine like wildfire. But since she'd said nothing to the local police except pointing out the bad guys, she had no idea how much they'd figured out about her and Gage.

She couldn't worry about all that. She was about to break some major rules. Gage wouldn't be happy about it, though he would understand. The Treasury Department would *really* not like it and was probably in the process of sending people to the hospital so they could be the first ones to question the survivors. She hoped they'd at least send Steele, so she'd have a familiar face to deal with.

For now, though, the government would have to wait. She had to talk to someone about all that had occurred in the last day and a half, and she didn't much care if that pissed somebody off.

Outside, she led her father away from the ambulance bay and driveway to a low brick wall that sat on the corner of the emergency wing. He swung her onto the wall as if she weighed nothing, as if she were a little girl again, waiting for news of her gravely injured mother. They'd sat in this exact spot, she remembered suddenly. Her, her father, Nicole and Ryan had waited in vain for good news. She prayed the same wouldn't be true today.

He jumped up beside her. "Did you pick this spot on purpose, baby?"

She stared at the silvery moon. "I'm not sure. Maybe."

"Do you want to talk about why three teams of NOPD officers, a station of firefighters, plus four federal agents that I *know* of found you and your fiancé in Joseph Stephano's warehouse full of counterfeiting equipment and several hundred thousand dollars in fake money?"

Her dad, Mr. Straight-to-the-Point. The thought made her smile. "Mmm. I'll get around to that."

So, in quiet, as calm as possible tones, she told him her story, beginning with Toni's suspicions at lunch yesterday and ending with her shooting Stephano in the leg, then later telling the jerkface he'd better stay where he was—hey, she had to throw herself in some kind of good light, since she figured her dad was going to be boiling mad at her for involving herself in a federal case uninvited and without a shred of experience.

When she finished, he gripped her hand in his. "You know, Rox. I think I'm a little relieved. There've been times I thought you were adopted."

She slapped his arm lightly. "Daddy!"

He squeezed her hand, his gaze zeroing in on hers. "And I'm also ticked as hell you insinuated yourself into a federal counterfeiting case with a notoriously dangerous mobster. You're an accountant, for God's sake, not a cop."

Hell, she'd been telling people that all night.

The idea forced a giggle past her lips. And once she started laughing, she couldn't stop. Part of her knew she'd become hysterical, battling misery and confusion with a smile and hoping desperately everything could just be the way it was before. The rest of her, the practical side she'd always embraced, knew her life had changed, irrevocably, forever. And this emotional outburst was just a release of tension. She'd have to deal with the changes soon. Back up some difficult decisions.

Her dad handed her his handkerchief. "Damn, Rox, the least you could have done was pay attention during my shooting lessons, then you'd have disabled Stephano a lot easier. You should have aimed mid-body."

She rolled her eyes. He sounded just like Gage. And she wasn't about to admit she'd aimed midbody and just luckily caught him in the leg. "What about Gage? Aren't you mad at him? He's the one who lied and tricked us all."

"Honey," he said in his patient, I'm-the-parent, let-me-handle-this tone, "that's his job. I'm upset for you, that he hurt you. He shouldn't have involved you in his life, and he'll hear from me about that, believe me. But you can't fault him for not telling you about his work."

"Oh, yes, I can. I can't marry him. I won't live that way."

"But you love him."

She paused before admitting, "Yes."

He said nothing for several long moments. "This is about your mother."

She swallowed. "Yes."

He looked up toward the moon. "Do you know how many nights I laid awake, blaming myself for her death?"

They'd had this talk a few times, when her grief had gotten the better of her and she'd said horrible, accusing words in her anger. She couldn't have spoken if her life depended on it. She hadn't intended to resurrect his grief, to open old wounds.

"Without you kids," he went on, "I probably wouldn't have made it. I would have drank myself to death or gone crazy. She was my life," he whispered. Then he cleared his throat. "But I knew Hope believed in me. She believed in what I did and who I was." He turned his head, and his watery gaze met hers. "She would have been disappointed if I'd given up, either before or after my job cost her her life."

"Daddy, I didn't mean—"

He kissed her forehead. "I know you didn't, pumpkin. I just want you to understand before you make a decision you could regret for the rest of your life." He held her by her shoulders, obviously fighting to bank his own regrets. "The guilt from losing her was incredible. Still is sometimes. But I knew I couldn't let evil and doubt and fear win. That's what you're doing, Rox. You're letting fear keep you from what, from who, you love most. You know I'll love you regardless, but I hope you consider carefully what you're throwing away."

The selfishness of her actions finally settled around her. She'd known she couldn't ask Gage to be someone he wasn't, but he'd offered to give up his career anyway. How hard had that been for him? How much had he been willing to give up to keep her? He wanted her beyond his instincts. He loved her beyond his reservations about the power of love.

And what he'd given her in return was immeasurably special as well. He'd given her confidence. In herself, in her abilities as a lover and a person. This weekend with Gage had helped her tap into a deep well of strength she hadn't known existed. One she might never have found without him. Without living as he did. Without allowing herself to explore the depths of their love and passion.

"You're pretty terrific," she said to her father.

He hugged her tight against his side. "You have

your moments, too, sweetie." He dropped to the ground, then assisted her down.

Her mother would have approved of Gage, she realized with sudden clarity. And if she could convince him she wasn't a selfish idiot and she'd love him forever, no matter what he did for a living, she just might live happily ever after. "I wouldn't cancel that tux fitting just yet."

He slid his arm around her waist as they walked back toward the emergency-room entrance. "That's my girl."

As they approached the door, a squad car squealed to a stop in the driveway. Her brother, Ryan, leaped from the driver's side, and her sister, Nicole, from the passenger's seat, then Steele and Toni darted out of the back seat. Before she'd managed to fully acknowledge their presence, they'd surrounded her. "What's going on? Is Gage okay? Why were you in a mobster's warehouse? Are you okay? Why are you wearing that outfit?"

The questions whirled around her until her head spun.

"Move that car, son," her father interjected. "This is the ambulance bay."

"Yes, sir," her brother said before rushing over to the car.

Nicole grabbed her shoulders, staring into her eyes. "You're wearing green contacts. Why are you wearing green contacts?"

Roxanne worked up a smile. "It's a long story, Nic."

Toni clutched her hand. To Roxanne's utter shock, tears were swimming in her friend's eyes. "I got him shot, didn't I? This is all my fault. You told me to go home. I just—"

"No. It's not your fault." She slid one arm around her friend and one around her sister. "We should know something soon."

"But what about you?" her sister insisted. "What's going on, Rox?"

"Not now."

Saying nothing, Nicole's gaze searched Roxanne's. Normally she couldn't have quieted her commanding sister with a firing squad if she was determined to uncover something, and with her and Toni double-teaming her, she'd never escape. But the effects of the surreal weekend she'd just lived through must have been obvious. So instead they both simply enfolded her in a hug, the shoulder holster beneath Nicole's jacket pressing against Roxanne's side. "Is Gage going to be okay?"

She sniffled, a strand of her sister's long blond hair escaping the bun she always wore tickling her nose. "I think so."

Nicole slid her arm around her shoulders as Ryan and Steele walked up. Nicole simply shook her head at the questions in her brother's eyes.

"You guys go ahead. I need a moment with Steele."

The mention of the large cowboy finally brought a smile to Toni's face. "Mmm. Hunk city. Remind me to tell you what a great kisser he is."

"You *kissed* Steele?"

Toni pursed her lips. "He said it was the only way he could shut me up." She waggled her fingers. "We'll see you inside."

And Toni hadn't slugged him? How had *that* happened?

Steele distracted her by leaning against the wall beside her. His ever-present black Stetson shadowed his face.

"Do you ever take that thing off?" she asked, frustrated that she couldn't see his eyes, and therefore, understand just exactly how pissed he was at her.

"Rarely," he responded shortly.

Wincing at his tone, she figured she might as well get straight to the point. "I'm sorry about earlier. Are you going to get in trouble with your boss?"

"I'm not gonna get a commendation."

She'd been afraid of that. Maybe she could talk to Gage's father for him. "Well, I—"

"You know, you and Antoinette suit each other." He tipped back his hat and glared down at her. "Both a passel of trouble."

Ah-ha. The man wasn't just out of sorts at her. "Did you call her that?"

"It's her name. 'Course I did."

So how had they gone from Antoinette—which Toni hated—to a hot kiss? Interesting.

A bit more cheerful, she linked arms with Steele and guided him into the emergency room. "I'll explain about Toni another time. Let's see what we can find out about Gage."

The presence of two highly respected detectives, one revered police captain and Toni—whose family money had built the cardiac wing—moved mountains. They received reports from the operating room and Gage's prognosis every fifteen minutes over the next two hours. He was stable, the injury to his shoulder not life-threatening, but they were concerned about permanent damage to the nerves.

Roxanne couldn't help but wonder what his prognosis would mean for his job. If the damage was permanent, would he have to retire? Was she getting what she wanted now that she'd finally realized how self-centered her wishes had been? Guilt and worry churned in her stomach.

Finally, a blue-scrub-clad doctor pushed through the door leading to the waiting room. "The family of Gage Dabon?" she asked.

Roxanne approached her. "I—"

"I'm his father." A tall, black-haired man, silver streaking his temples and dressed in an expensive-looking blue suit, whom Roxanne hadn't even seen in the waiting room until this moment, walked toward the doctor.

When his gaze slid to Roxanne, she nearly gasped at the resemblance to Gage. *This is what Gage will look like in thirty years.*

She supposed he *had* gotten his in-charge butt on a plane and come down.

He held out his hand to her. "Colin MacDonald." He smiled—a smile just as enticing and confident as Gage's. "I believe we spoke on the phone earlier."

She shook his hand, wondering about the differences in their last names and working through the unexpected charm she found. She'd expected to resent him, or at the very least find him drab and uninteresting. Thankfully, her sister took over the introductions of everyone else, then they all turned to the doctor.

Roxanne held her sister's and brother's hands. And she held her breath.

Though her eyes were tired, the doctor smiled. "Mr. Dabon is fine and beginning to wake up. I expect him to make a full recovery."

Roxanne embraced her family, Toni and Steele, then, what the hell, she hugged Gage's father. He seemed surprised at first, holding himself stiff, then he squeezed her tight and whispered, "Thank you for taking care of him."

She nodded and blinked back tears.

The doctor touched her arm. "Roxanne?" When Roxanne nodded, she said, "He's asking for you."

She started off, then looked back at Gage's father. "Come on, Colin."

He joined her, and they followed the doctor down the hall and to the elevator. "You're due for a debriefing."

She glanced at her watch. "You held back for three whole minutes, Colin. I'm proud of you."

"I bet you frustrate the hell out of Gage sometimes."

"I'm learning, sir."

As the elevator came to a halt, the doctor glanced curiously over her shoulder at them.

"It's been a long night, Doctor, and I don't think I thanked you for saving my fiancé's life."

"You're welcome." The doctor held her hand across the elevator doors and let Roxanne and Colin proceed her into the hall. "He should be allowed to go home in a day or two."

"How about the others? Do you know anything about them?" As much as she detested Stephano and the pain he had caused her and countless others throughout his miserable life, neither did she want his death on her conscience. And poor Clark Mettles.

Somehow she sensed he'd taken a wrong turn early in his life and had no idea how to go the other way.

"I'm sorry, I don't," the doctor said.

"The two bodyguards were DOA," Colin said. "Mettles is still in surgery, though he looks like he'll make it. Stephano will live. Hopefully a long life in prison."

The doctor didn't ask how her patient's father knew more about what was going on in the hospital than she did. No doubt she'd dealt with the police at times in the past and knew questions didn't guarantee answers.

She turned the handle on a door halfway down the hall. "Talk to him. It will help him come out of the anesthesia." She laid her hand briefly on Roxanne's shoulder. "And let me know if I can do anything for you."

Roxanne squeezed her hand. "Thank you."

As the doctor left, Colin pushed the door, which swung open, and Roxanne gasped at the sight of Gage, pale and still against the sheets, with tubes twisting from his arms. "They'll take the tubes out soon. Don't let them upset you." He urged her to the side of the bed.

Swallowing, she sank into the chair at his side. Her body trembled as she captured his hand in both of hers. "Gage?" His hand twitched, so she went on. "Your father and I are here. We're so glad you're going to be okay." With her thumb, she stroked the back of his hand and continued talking to him quietly, soothingly.

"Open your eyes, Gage," his father said suddenly, his voice loud and commanding.

To her surprise and irritation, Gage's eyes fluttered,

then opened fully. His gaze met hers, then his eyes widened as he saw his father. He opened his mouth, but no sound emerged.

"Don't try to talk," she said, rising to brush a lock of hair off his forehead.

He didn't need to say anything. The look in his eyes spoke volumes.

Relief. Happiness. *Love.*

She could hardly believe she'd even considered rejecting those gifts.

His eyes closed again.

"Gage?" She glanced at Colin. "Isn't he supposed to stay awake?"

"It may take a while." He sat in the chair next to her, drawing her back down, sliding his arm across her shoulders. "Why don't you rest? I'll wake you when he does."

"Okay." As long as Gage knew she was with him she supposed she could rest a minute.

But as she leaned against Colin, a nurse walked into the room. "Ms. Lewis?" She extended a plastic bag to Roxanne. "These are Mr. Dabon's personal items."

Roxanne laid the bag in her lap. "Thank you."

"I also found this in his pocket," she said, placing a diamond and emerald ring in her palm. "I was afraid it might get lost if I didn't hand it to you personally."

Tears of happiness crowding her throat, Roxanne closed her fist around her engagement ring.

The nurse left, and Roxanne's gaze locked on Gage's face. She leaned forward and kissed the back of his hand as she slid the ring on her finger, then leaned her head against Colin's broad shoulder.

She closed her eyes with a smile on her face.

GAGE STRUGGLED with the window. He tapped on the pane with his fist. "It's stuck," he whispered.

At the bottom of the ladder, Steele pushed back his Stetson. "Why can't you just go in the front door?" he whispered back angrily.

"I told you," he said as he climbed down. "I want to surprise her."

"MacDonald is going to fry my ass for busting you out of the hospital."

"I'll put in a good word for you. Now up you go. Just crack the window. I'll open it the rest of the way."

"I'm gonna get fired," Steele grumbled, though he started up the ladder.

"Maybe, but you'll get other offers."

Gage watched his new friend work his way to Roxanne's bedroom window, wondering how he was going to slither his way through without using his injured shoulder—or alarming her brother, who he understood was sleeping on the couch downstairs. His father and others were still rounding up Stephano's men, and they felt Roxanne needed protection until they were sure everyone was accounted for.

Steele climbed back down, dropping to the grass beside Gage. "All set, Romeo," he said, extending his arm in invitation. "I still don't understand why this couldn't wait until tomorrow."

After all he and Roxanne had been through in the last two days, Gage had no intention of waiting another moment for their future to begin. According to his father and hers, Roxanne had left the hospital wearing a ring on the third finger of her left hand. If that wasn't a positive sign, his years of detective work had been a complete disaster. He had no idea what had changed in the last several hours, but he intended to find out as soon as possible.

He looked up the long length of the ladder, to the darkened bedroom and thought of the woman who lay beyond. "You will someday."

Holding on with one hand and shifting his sling for better balance, he started up. At the top, he used his good hand to slide the window up farther, and deciding to go headfirst, he leaned forward, so his stomach lay across the sill.

"Hold it right there, buddy."

Gage jerked his head up. Wearing a long NOPD T-shirt, Roxanne stood a few feet from him, a pistol pointed at his head.

Okay, maybe she'd taken the ring, intending to hock it.

"Gage, what are you doing here?" she asked, rushing toward him.

"What are *you* doing *here*? I thought you'd be at the hospital when I woke up."

With her help, he managed to slide the rest of the way into the room. "Your father told me you'd sleep through the night. I argued that I still wanted to stay, but he insisted I come home and get some rest. Have you ever won an argument with that man?"

He thought about their discussion on his and Roxanne's engagement. "Just once."

She glared at him. "I thought you were one of Stephano's goons. And how in the world did you get out of the hospital? The doctor said you'd be there another few days."

"Steele rescued me."

She stuck her head out the window. "Good grief." She waved at the man below. "Move that ladder before somebody sees it and calls the cops," she called down.

Smiling broadly, Steele saluted. "Yes, ma'am."

She closed the window and turned back, setting the gun on her nightstand.

"That's my gun," he said in wonder, thinking mere days ago he'd never have imagined a gun in her hand, much less her being prepared to use it on an intruder.

"Your father gave it to me as he shoved me out of the hospital." She crossed her arms over her chest, and the ring on her finger glinted in the moonlight.

She's still wearing it. This plan is going to work.

"My brother is downstairs, you know," she went on. "You're lucky you didn't get shot."

He stroked her cheek, so glad to be this close to her, to smell her and feel her, he didn't much care if she was angry with him. "Again."

"You look pale."

"I feel fine."

She suddenly threw her arms around his neck, careful not to bump the sling holding his arm. "You scared me to death."

He laughed. "*Me?* You're the one who charged from behind those crates, guns blazing, holding off Stephano and his henchmen." He kissed her temple. "Let's avoid working together in the future." Yikes. Bad word. They did have a future, didn't they? He didn't want to acknowledge how nervous he was about asking that question.

She leaned back. "You've got a deal. It had its moments, but I'll stick to accounting, thank you. You can handle saving the world from now on."

He drew a deep breath. "I can?"

"With my full support and undying love and devotion." She kissed his lips softly. "I never should have asked you to choose, Gage. I bless the day I met you. You make my life special, and I don't want you to change anything."

He looked into her eyes, the love and resolve for him. Only for him. "I would do anything for you. Whether I was a financier, a farmer, or a cop, I wouldn't let you go. But thank you for accepting me. I understand how hard it was for you."

She smiled. "My dad helped."

"Mmm. Remarkable guy. He was very supportive when I quit my job earlier. He offered me a detective badge at NOPD."

She gripped his neck. "When you—"

"Well, technically, I guess I retired. My boss was there, so it seemed fitting, and since my father blew my cover by showing up and announcing who he was, it would have taken some delicate maneuvering to straighten everything out later. He even admitted he was a bit relieved to have me out of the undercover business. He didn't really care for the unsettling trip to the emergency room."

"Is that what he said?"

"Practically word for word. Dear ol' dad is such a sentimentalist."

"He can be kind of charming."

"Charming?"

"He has quite an effect on a woman."

He lifted his eyebrows. "He does, huh?"

She kissed him. "Now I know where you get it."

If he wasn't mistaken, he thought his future wife had just admitted a spark of attraction to his father. He'd have to think about that. But later. "Let's—"

"Why do you two have different last names, anyway?"

Since the last name of someone else was on his mind, that was as perfect a lead-in to his question as any. "I changed mine to one of my mother's old family names when I entered the department. His position is fairly visible, and we didn't want anyone outside the Secret Service to know we were related."

While she processed that, he reached behind his head, taking hold of her left hand with his, then crouching in front of her. The engagement ring he'd slid on her finger so many months ago was back, and he had to swallow a lump of emotional gratitude before he could speak. He looked up at her, thinking how lovely and delicate she looked in the pale glow of dawn. "How do you feel about my last name? Sharing it, I mean?"

Tears filling her eyes, she squeezed his hand. "I'd love to share it."

He stood. "Great. Let's elope."

Her mouth fell open. "Elope? We have to get you back to the hospital. You need rest."

"I'll get it. I don't have to report to the station for two months." He started to swing her into his arms, then remembered that was impossible in his present condition. He slid his arm around her waist instead, the warmth of her body seeping into his as he led her back to the window. "I have plenty of time to recuperate. How does Martinique sound?"

"You're crazy. We can't just run off the in middle of the night."

He lifted the window and peeked out to be sure Steele was still at his post and he hadn't followed Roxanne's advice about moving the ladder. This was going to be a short escape if the agent had deserted him. But he was there, giving Gage the thumbs-up sign.

"You don't like Martinique?" he asked Roxanne casually. He'd known her sense of responsibility was going to make this a bit of a struggle, but he wasn't letting another night pass without making sure she was his completely and forever. "We could go somewhere else. I just picked a place where we wouldn't be required to wear too many clothes."

She groaned, then pressed her lips to the side of his neck. "We can not wear clothes right here, near the hospital."

He glanced back at the bed. Tempting, but he had a judge waiting. "They have hospitals in Martinique."

She dug in her heels as he climbed out the window. "Your dad is expecting me in the morning for my debriefing."

"We'll call him."

"My brother."

"We'll call him, too." Smiling, he extended his hand to her. "Come on, Rox. What are you waiting for?"

She laid her hand in his without hesitation. "I suddenly can't think of a single thing."

Is your man too good to be true?

Hot, gorgeous AND romantic?
If so, he could be a Harlequin® Blaze™ series cover model!

Our grand-prize winners will receive a trip for two to New York City to
shoot the cover of a Blaze novel, and will stay at the luxurious Plaza Hotel.
Plus, they'll receive $500 U.S. spending money!
The runner-up winners will receive $200 U.S.
to spend on a romantic dinner for two.

It's easy to enter!

In 100 words or less, tell us what makes your boyfriend or spouse a true romantic
and the perfect candidate for the cover of a Blaze novel, and include in your submission
two photos of this potential cover model.

All entries must include the written submission of the contest entrant, two photographs of the model
candidate and the Official Entry Form and Publicity Release forms completed in full and signed by
both the model candidate and the contest entrant. Harlequin, along with the experts at
Elite Model Management, will select a winner.

For photo and complete Contest details, please refer to the Official Rules on the next page. All entries
will become the property of Harlequin Enterprises Ltd. and are not returnable.

Please visit www.blazecovermodel.com to download a copy of the Official Entry Form and
Publicity Release Form or send a request to one of the addresses below.

Please mail your entry to: **Harlequin Blaze Cover Model Search**

In U.S.A.	In Canada
P.O. Box 9069	P.O. Box 637
Buffalo, NY	Fort Erie, ON
14269-9069	L2A 5X3

No purchase necessary. Contest open to Canadian and U.S. residents who are 18 and over.
Void where prohibited. Contest closes September 30, 2003.

HARLEQUIN BLAZE COVER MODEL SEARCH CONTEST 3569 OFFICIAL RULES
NO PURCHASE NECESSARY TO ENTER

1. To enter, submit two (2) 4" x 6" photographs of a boyfriend or spouse (who must be 18 years of age or older) taken no later than three (3) months from the time of entry: a close-up, waist up, shirtless photograph; and a fully clothed, full-length photograph, then, tell us, in 100 words or fewer, why he should be a Harlequin Blaze cover model and how he is romantic. Your complete "entry" must include: (i) your essay, (ii) the Official Entry Form and Publicity Release Form printed below completed and signed by you (as "Entrant"), (iii) the photographs (with your hand-written name, address and phone number, and your model's name, address and phone number on the back of each photograph), and (iv) the Publicity Release Form and Photograph Representation Form printed below completed and signed by your model (as "Model"), and should be sent via first-class mail to either: Harlequin Blaze Cover Model Search Contest 3569, P.O. Box 9069, Buffalo, NY, 14269-9069, or Harlequin Blaze Cover Model Search Contest 3569, P.O. Box 637, Fort Erie, Ontario L2A 5X3. All submissions must be in English and be received no later than September 30, 2003. Limit: one entry per person, household or organization. **Purchase or acceptance of a product offer does not improve your chances of winning.** All entry requirements must be strictly adhered to for eligibility and to ensure fairness among entries.

2. Ten (10) Finalist submissions (photographs and essays) will be selected by a panel of judges consisting of members of the Harlequin editorial, marketing and public relations staff, as well as a representative from Elite Model Management (Toronto) Inc., based on the following criteria:

Aptness/Appropriateness of submitted photographs for a Harlequin Blaze cover—70%
Originality of Essay—20%
Sincerity of Essay—10%

In the event of a tie, duplicate finalists will be selected. The photographs submitted by finalists will be posted on the Harlequin website no later than November 15, 2003 (at www.blazecovermodel.com), and viewers may vote, in rank order, on their favorite(s) to assist in the panel of judges' final determination of the Grand Prize and Runner-up winning entries based on the above judging criteria. All decisions of the judges are final.

3. All entries become the property of Harlequin Enterprises Ltd. and none will be returned. Any entry may be used for future promotional purposes. Elite Model Management (Toronto) Inc. and/or its partners, subsidiaries and affiliates operating as "Elite Model Management" will have access to all entries including all personal information, and may contact any Entrant and/or Model in its sole discretion for their own business purposes. Harlequin and Elite Model Management (Toronto) Inc. are separate entities with no legal association or partnership whatsoever having no power to bind or obligate the other or create any expressed or implied obligation or responsibility on behalf of the other, such that Harlequin shall not be responsible in any way for any acts or omissions of Elite Model Management (Toronto) Inc. or its partners, subsidiaries and affiliates in connection with the Contest or otherwise and Elite Model Management shall not be responsible in any way for any acts or omissions of Harlequin or its partners, subsidiaries and affiliates in connection with the contest or otherwise.

4. All Entrants and Models must be residents of the U.S. or Canada, be 18 years of age or older, and have no prior criminal convictions. The contest is not open to any Model that is a professional model and/or actor in any capacity at the time of the entry. Contest void wherever prohibited by law; all applicable laws and regulations apply. Any litigation within the Province of Quebec regarding the conduct or organization of a publicity contest may be submitted to the Régie des alcools, des courses et des jeux for a ruling, and any litigation regarding the awarding of a prize may be submitted to the Régie only for the purpose of helping the parties reach a settlement. Employees and immediate family members of Harlequin Enterprises Ltd., D.L. Blair, Inc., Elite Model Management (Toronto) Inc. and their parents, affiliates, subsidiaries and all other agencies, entities and persons connected with the use, marketing or conduct of this Contest are not eligible to enter. Acceptance of any prize offered constitutes permission to use Entrants' and Models' names, essay submissions, photographs or other likenesses for the purposes of advertising, trade, publication and promotion on behalf of Harlequin Enterprises Ltd., its parent, affiliates, subsidiaries, assigns and other authorized entities involved in the judging and promotion of the contest without further compensation to any Entrant or Model, unless prohibited by law.

5. Finalists will be determined no later than October 30, 2003. Prize Winners will be determined no later than January 31, 2004. Grand Prize Winners (consisting of winning Entrant and Model) will be required to sign and return Affidavit of Eligibility/Release of Liability and Model Release forms within thirty (30) days of notification. Non-compliance with this requirement and within the specified time period will result in disqualification and an alternate will be selected. Any prize notification returned as undeliverable will result in the awarding of the prize to an alternate set of winners. All travelers (or parent/legal guardian of a minor) must execute the Affidavit of Eligibility/Release of Liability prior to ticketing and must possess required travel documents (e.g. valid photo ID) where applicable. Travel dates specified by Sponsor but no later than May 30, 2004.

6. Prizes: One (1) Grand Prize—the opportunity for the Model to appear on the cover of a paperback book from the Harlequin Blaze series, and a 3 day/2 night trip for two (Entrant and Model) to New York, NY for the photo shoot of Model which includes round-trip coach air transportation from the commercial airport nearest the winning Entrant's home to New York, NY, (or, in lieu of air transportation, $100 cash payable to Entrant and Model, if the winning Entrant's home is within 250 miles of New York, NY), hotel accommodations (double occupancy) at the Plaza Hotel and $500 cash spending money payable to Entrant and Model, (approximate prize value: $8,000), and one (1) Runner-up Prize of $200 cash payable to Entrant and Model for a romantic dinner for two (approximate prize value: $200). Prizes are valued in U.S. currency. Prizes consist of only those items listed as part of the prize. No substitution of prize(s) permitted by winners. All prizes are awarded jointly to the Entrant and Model of the winning entries, and are not severable - prizes and obligations may not be assigned or transferred. Any change to the Entrant and/or Model of the winning entries will result in disqualification and an alternate will be selected. Taxes on prize are the sole responsibility of winners. Any and all expenses and/or items not specifically described as part of the prize are the sole responsibility of winners. Harlequin Enterprises Ltd. and D.L. Blair, Inc., their parents, affiliates, and subsidiaries are not responsible for errors in printing of Contest entries and/or game pieces. No responsibility is assumed for lost, stolen, late, illegible, incomplete, inaccurate, non-delivered, postage due or misdirected mail or entries. In the event of printing or other errors which may result in unintended prize values or duplication of prizes, all affected game pieces or entries shall be null and void.

7. Winners will be notified by mail. For winners' list (available after March 31, 2004), send a self-addressed, stamped envelope to: Harlequin Blaze Cover Model Search Contest 3569 Winners, P.O. Box 4200, Blair, NE 68009-4200, or refer to the Harlequin website (at www.blazecovermodel.com).

Contest sponsored by Harlequin Enterprises Ltd., P.O. Box 9042, Buffalo, NY 14269-9042.

HBCVRMODEL2

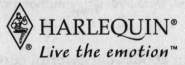

You like
Harlequin Duets™

You'll LOVE

HARLEQUIN
flipside™

It's fun, witty and full of insightful moments you *know* you can relate to!

"It's chick-lit with the romance and happily-ever-after ending that Harlequin is known for."
—*USA TODAY* bestselling author Millie Criswell, author of *Staying Single*, October 2003

"Even though our heroine may take a few false steps while finding her way, she does it with wit and humor."
—Dorien Kelly, author of *Do-Over*, November 2003

Don't miss the exciting launch next month!

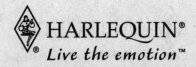

HARLEQUIN®
Live the emotion™

Visit us at www.harlequinflipside.com

HFDUETS

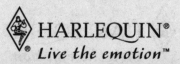